SUSAN HILL

Susan Hill has been a professional writer for over fifty years. Her books have won awards and prizes including the Whitbread, the John Llewellyn Rhys and the Somerset Maugham, and have been shortlisted for the Booker. Her novels include *Strange Meeting*, *I'm the King of the Castle*, *In the Springtime of the Year* and *The Mist in the Mirror*. She has also published autobiographical works and collections of short stories, as well as the Simon Serrailler series of crime novels. The play of her ghost story *The Woman in Black* is one of the longest-running in the history of London's West End. In 2020 she was awarded a damehood (DBE) for services to literature. She has two adult daughters and lives in north Norfolk.

## ALSO BY SUSAN HILL

### THE SIMON SERRAILLER CASES

*The Various Haunts of Men*
*The Pure in Heart*
*The Risk of Darkness*
*The Vows of Silence*
*The Shadows in the Street*
*The Betrayal of Trust*
*A Question of Identity*
*The Soul of Discretion*
*The Comforts of Home*
*The Benefit of Hindsight*
*A Change of Circumstance*

### FICTION

*Gentleman and Ladies*
*A Change for the Better*
*I'm the King of the Castle*
*The Albatross and Other Stories*
*Strange Meeting*
*The Bird of Night*
*A Bit of Singing and Dancing*
*In the Springtime of the Year*
*The Woman in Black*
*Air and Angels*
*The Mist in the Mirror*
*Mrs de Winter*
*The Service of Clouds*
*The Boy Who Taught the Beekeeper to Read*
*The Man in the Picture*
*The Beacon*
*The Small Hand*
*A Kind Man*
*Black Sheep*
*The Travelling Bag*
*From the Heart*

### NON-FICTION

*The Magic Apple Tree*
*Family*
*Howards End is on the Landing*

### FOR CHILDREN

*Can It be True?*
*The Glass Angels*
*The Battle for Gullywith*

SUSAN HILL

# Dolly

VINTAGE

1 3 5 7 9 10 8 6 4 2

Vintage is part of the Penguin Random House group of companies
whose addresses can be found at global.penguinrandomhouse.com

Penguin
Random House
UK

First published by Vintage in 2023
First published in Great Britain by Profile Books in 2012

penguin.co.uk/vintage

Typeset in 11/16pt Janson Text LT Std by Jouve (UK), Milton Keynes
Printed and bound in Great Britain by Clays Ltd, Elcograf S.p.A.

The authorised representative in the EEA is Penguin Random House
Ireland, Morrison Chambers, 32 Nassau Street, Dublin D02 YH68

A CIP catalogue record for this book is
available from the British Library

ISBN 9781529913385

Penguin Random House is committed to a sustainable future
for our business, our readers and our planet. This book is made
from Forest Stewardship Council® certified paper.

# IYOT LOCK

A<small>N AUTUMN</small> night and the fens stretch for miles, open and still. It is dark, until the full moon slides from behind a cloud and over the huddle of grey stone which is Iyot Lock. The hamlet straddles a cross roads between flat field and flat field, with its squat church on the east side, hard by Iyot House and the graveyard in between. On the west side, a straggle of cottages leads to Iyot Farm, whose flat fields bleed into the flat fens with no apparent boundary.

It is rare for a night here to be so still. The wind from the sea keens and whistles, though that sea is some miles away. Birds cry their eerie cries.

And then, a slight, thin movement of the air, from inland. It skims over the low dykes and watery ditches, rattles the dry reeds and rushes, rustles the grasses along the roadside.

It strengthens to a low wind and the wind weaves through the few trees in the churchyard and taps the branches of the creeper against the windows of Iyot House.

Nobody hears, for the house is empty and surely the sleepers in the churchyard are not disturbed.

The grasses whisper, the wind moves among the gravestones. And somewhere just about here, by the low wall, another sound, not like the grass but like paper rustling. But there is no paper.

The creeper scrapes the windowpanes. The moon slips out, silvering the glass.

The wind prowls around Iyot Lock, shifting the branches, stirring the grasses, swaying faintly, and from somewhere nearby, hidden or even buried, the sound of rustling.

# PART ONE

# I

It was a November afternoon when I returned to Iyot Lock and saw that nothing had changed. It was as I recalled it from forty years earlier, the sky as vast, the fen as flat, the river as dark and secretly flowing as it had been in my mind and memory. There had sometimes been sunshine, the river had gleamed and glinted, the larks had soared and sung on a June day, but this was how I knew it best, this landscape of dun and steel, with the sky falling in on my head and the wind keening and the ghosts and will-o'-the-wisps haunting my childhood nights.

I drove over Hoggett's bridge, seeing the water flow sluggishly beneath, and across the flat straight road, past the old lock keeper's cottage, abandoned now, but then the home of the lock keeper with a wen on his nose and one glass eye, who looked after his sluices and his eel traps in sullen silence. I used to steer clear of Mr Norry, of whom I was mortally, superstitiously afraid. But the blackened wood and brick cottage was empty and the roof fallen in. As I went by, a great bird with ragged wings rose out of it and flapped away, low over the water.

I could see far ahead to where the fen met the sky and the tower of Iyot Church, and then the house itself shimmered into view, hazy at first in the veils of rain, then larger, clearer, darker. The only trees for miles were the trees around the churchyard and those close to Iyot House, shading it from sight of the road, though few people, now as ever, were likely to pass by.

I parked beside the church wall and got out. The rain was a fine drizzle lying like cobwebs on my hair and the shoulders of my coat. Mine was the only car, so unless she had parked at the house, I was the first to arrive. That did not surprise me.

I pushed open the heavy greened wood of the gate and walked up the path to the church door. Crumpled chicken wire had been used to cover the arch and keep out birds, but it had loosened and old twigs and bits of blackened straw poked through where they had still managed to nest. I lifted the iron handle, twisted it and the door creaked open. The cold inside the porch made me catch my breath. Beyond the inner door, inside the church itself, it was more intense still and smelled of damp stone and mould. It seemed to be the cold of centuries and to seep into my bones as I stood there.

I did not remember anything about the church, though I was sure I must have been there on Sundays, with my aunt – I had a folk memory of the hard polished pews against my bony little backside and legs, for I had been a thin child. It was dull and pale, with uninteresting memorial tablets and clear glass windows that let the silvery daylight in onto the grey floor. Even the Lion and Unicorn, the only touch of colour in the church, painted in red and faded gold and blue on a wooden panel, and which might have taken the attention of a small boy, was quite unfamiliar. Perhaps my memories had been of another church altogether.

I wandered about, half expecting to hear the door open and see her standing there, but no one came and my footsteps were solitary on the stone floor.

The lights did not come on when I clicked the switch and the church was dim in the sullen November afternoon. I made my way out again, but as I stood looking out at the path and the graveyard, I had a strange and quite urgent sense that I ought to do something, that I was needed, that I was the one person who could rescue – rescue what? Who? I could not remember when I had had such an anxious feeling and as I walked out, it became stronger, almost as if someone were tugging at my sleeve and begging me to help them. But there was no one. The churchyard was empty and it felt desolate in the gathering dusk, with the brooding sky overhead, though it was only just after three o'clock.

I shook myself, to be rid of the inexplicable feeling and walked briskly to the car and drove the short distance to the house, the back and chimneys of which were hard to the road. There were the wooden gates, which I remembered well. If I opened them I could swing into the yard and park behind the scullery and outhouses, but the gate was locked and seemingly barred on the inside, so I returned to the lay-by beside the church and set out to walk back along the deserted lane to Iyot House. I glanced down the road but there was no sight of a car, even far away, no moving dot in the distance.

And then, it was as if something were tugging at my sleeve, though I felt nothing. I was being urged to return to the churchyard and I could not disobey, whatever was asking me to go there needed something – needed me? What did it want me to do and why? Where exactly was I to go?

I turned again, feeling considerably annoyed but

unable to resist, and the moment I set off I sensed that this was right, and that who or whatever wanted me there was relieved and pleased with me. We all like to please by doing the thing we are being asked, in spite of our misgivings, and so I retraced my steps briskly the hundred yards to the lych gate. That was not quite far enough. I must go through and into the church-yard. By now the dark was gathering fast and I could barely see my way, but there were still streaks of light in the sky to the west and it was not a large area. I moved slowly among the gravestones. It was almost as if I were playing the old childhood game of Hide and Seek, one in which the inner sense was saying 'Cold' 'Cold' 'Warm' 'Very Warm'.

It was as I neared three gravestones that were set against the low wall at the back that the sense of urgency became very strong. I went to each one. All were ancient, moss and lichen-covered and the names and dates were no longer visible. Even as I got near to the first I felt a peculiar electric shock of heat, fol-lowed immediately by a sense of release. This was it. I was there. But where? Wherever I was meant to be? Then by whom, and why?

I stood still. The wind was keening, the darkness shrinking in to swallow me. I was not exactly afraid but I was uneasy and bewildered. And then I heard it. It seemed to be coming from the ground in front of a gravestone. I squatted down and listened. The moan of the wind was blocked out by the wall there, and it was very still. At first I could not make it out but after a few moments, I thought it sounded as if something was rustling, a dry sound, like that made by the wind in the reed beds, but softer and fainter. It came from under the grass, under the earth. A rustling, as if some-one were . . .

No, I could not tell. I stayed for some minutes and the rustling came again and again, and each time it made me feel as one feels when a name one has for-gotten is almost, almost on the tip of the tongue. I knew the sound, I knew what was making it, I knew why . . . but it hovered just out of reach, like the elusive name. I knew and then did not know, I remembered – but then it was gone. I waited for a few more minutes. Nothing else happened, I heard nothing else and not least because by this time I was thoroughly chilled. The east wind was whistling across the fen even more strongly and I left the churchyard and returned to Iyot House.

It was in pitch darkness and the wind had got up even more in that short time and was dashing the trees against the walls and rattling the ivy. Stupidly I had not brought a torch and had to edge my way through the gate and up the narrow path between thickly overgrown shrubs to the front door. I had the key ready and to my surprise the lock was smooth and opened at a turn. I felt about for a switch – there was none in the porch but once inside the hall I found the panel of them to my left. The hall, staircase and narrow passageway were lit, though the bulbs were quite dim. But at once, the past came rushing towards me as I not only saw but smelled the inside of the house where I had once been a small boy on occasional and always strange visits. The pictures on the wall, one of a half-draped woman by a rock pool, another of sheep in the snow, and two portraits whose eyes pierced me and then seemed to follow me, as they always had, reminded me of the past, the feel of the polished floor beneath the rug at my feet, the great brass dinner gong, the once-polished and gleaming banister, now filmed and dull, reminded me, and the silent grandfather clock, the frieze of brown carnations running along the wallpaper, the dark velveteen curtain hanging on a rod across the drawing room door, all these things reminded me . . . As I looked round I was eight years old again and in Iyot House for the first time, anxious, wary, full of half-fears, jumping at my own shadow as it glided beside me up the stairs.

But I was not afraid of anything there that late afternoon, merely affected by the atmosphere of sadness

11

and emptiness. Iyot House had never been full of light and fun but it was not a gloomy house either and people who had lived there had looked after me as best they knew, and even loved me – though perhaps I had little sense of it as a boy. I had been afraid of shadows and darkness, of sudden sounds, of spiders and bats but I had never believed Iyot House had any ghosts or malign forces hanging about within its walls, at least not until . . .

I stopped with one foot on the stairs . . . until what? It was teasing me again, that sense of something just out of reach, almost remembered but then fluttering off just as I grasped it.

Until something had happened? Or was it to do with some*one*?

It was no good. I could not remember, it had danced away, to tantalise me yet again.

I went round the house, putting on the lights as I did so, and each room came alive at the touch of the switch, bedrooms, dressing rooms, bathrooms, their furniture and curtains and carpets exactly as I had known them, faded now and dusty, with the smell of all rooms into which fresh air had not come through an opened window, for years. I did not feel anything much, not sadness or fondness, just a certain muted nostalgia.

And then I climbed the last steep, short flight of stairs to the attics and at once I felt an odd fluttering sensation in my chest, as though I were reaching somewhere important, where I might at last be able to recall the incident that was nudging at my memory.

This was familiar. This had been my territory. These small rooms with their tiny, iron-latched windows, the narrow single bed, the bare floorboards, had been where I slept, dreamed, thought, played . . . and where I had first encountered Leonora.

I made my way to the room that had been mine. It was the same, and yet quite different, because though the furniture was as I recalled, there were, of course, none of my clothes, toys, games or books, nothing that had made it personal to me, brought it alive. It also seemed far smaller than I had remembered – but, of course, I am a man of six feet two and I was a small boy when I had been here last. I sat on the bed. The mattress was the same, soft but with the springs beneath poking through here and there. I felt them again, digging into my thinly fleshed young back. The wicker chair was almost too small for me to sit in, the window seat narrow and hard. I remembered the wallpaper with its frieze of beige roses, the iron fireplace with the scrolled canopy, the tall cupboard set deep into the wall.

The cupboard. It was something about the cupboard; something in it or that had happened beside it?

13

I did not want to open it, and though I felt foolish, my hand hovered on the latch for several seconds, and my heart started to beat fast. I did not remember anything except that my mounting distress meant the game was over, I was 'hot'.

I did open it, of course. It was empty, the shelves dusty. It went some way back and as I took a couple of deep breaths and felt calmer, I reached up and ran my hand along the shelves. Nothing. There was nothing there at all, nothing until I reached the top shelf, so far from me when I was a boy that I had to stand on the stool to reach it, but now easily accessible. Still nothing.

I shook myself, and was about to close the cupboard door when I heard it – a very soft rustling, as if someone were stirring their hand about in crisp tissue paper, perhaps as they unpacked a parcel. It stopped. I opened the door wide again. The rustling was a little louder. I got the old stool, stood on it and felt the top shelf of the cupboard to the very back, where my hand touched the wall. Nothing. It was totally and completely empty.

Nevertheless, there was the sound again, and although it was no louder, it seemed more urgent and agitated.

I lost my nerve, closed the cupboard and fled, running down the stairs to the hall. When I stopped and got my breath back, I listened. The wind was whistling down the chimney and lifting the rug on the floor, but I could no longer hear even the faintest sound of paper rustling.

I went into the sitting room, thinking to wait for her there but it had such a damp and chill, and the fireplace was full of rubble, so I retreated, switched out the lights and locked the front door. The wind seemed to pare the skin off my face as I turned into the lane and I hastened to get into the car. I would drive back to the market town and my small, warm, comfortable hotel. It was obvious that she was not going to come to Iyot House – perhaps she had never intended it.

But I knew that even if she did come, she would not remember anything. We blot out bad things from our minds and especially when they have been bad things we ourselves have done, in childhood perhaps most of all.

A chill mist was smothering the fen and veils of it writhed in front of the headlights as I drove away. I would be glad to get to the Lion at Cold Eeyle, and a good malt whisky by the fire, even more glad to have the whole thing done with at the solicitor's the next morning. Would Leonora turn up there? I had no doubt that she would. The prospect of inheriting something was just what would bring her up here, as nothing else had ever done – I knew she had not visited Aunt Kestrel in forty years, but then she had lived abroad for the most part, following her mother's example in marrying several times. I did not know if she had any children but I doubted it.

The Lion was snug and welcoming, after an unpleasant ten-mile drive through the swirling fog. My room was at the top of the house, down some winding corridors. I spruced up and returned to the bar, a whisky and the log fire.

I ate a good dinner and went to bed early. The place was quiet and when I had got my key, the receptionist said that I was the only person staying. The meeting at the solicitor's was at ten, in his Cold Eeyle office.

I thought about Aunt Kestrel that night, after I had read a dozen pages and put out the light. I had barely known her, wished I had talked to her more about the family and the past she could have told me so much about. She had housed a stiff, shy small boy and a wayward girl when she had no knowledge of children, what they wanted or needed. She could have refused but she had not, feeling strongly, as her generation did, about family ties and family duty. Of course, it had never occurred to me as a boy that she was probably lonely, widowed young, childless, and living in that

16

bleak and isolated house with only the moaning wind, the fogs and rain for company, other than sour Mrs Mullen.

I fell asleep thinking about the two of them, and about Leonora and how anxious I had been about the way she behaved, when we were children, how she had seemed so careless about bringing wrath down on her own head and curses on the house in general.

I woke and put on the bedside lamp. It was deathly quiet. Obviously the fog had not lifted but was swaddling the land, deadening every sound. Not that there would be many. Cars did not drive around Cold Eeyle at night, people did not walk the streets.

I was about to pick up my book and read a few more pages to lull myself off again, when my ears picked up a slight and distant sound. I knew what it was at once, and it acted like a pick stabbing through the ice of memory. It was the sound of crying. I got up and opened the window. The taste of the fog came into my mouth and its damp web touched my skin. But through its felted layers, from far away, I heard it again, half in my own head, half out there, and then everything came vividly back, the scene with Leonora in Aunt Kestrel's sitting room, her rage, the crack of the china head against the fireplace, my own fear, prompting my heart to leap in my chest. All, all of it I remembered – no, I re-lived, my heart pounding again, as I stood at the window and through the fog-blanketed darkness heard the sound again.

Deep under the earth, inside its cardboard coffin, shrouded in the layers of white paper, the china doll with the jagged open crevasse in its skull was crying.

# PART TWO

PART TWO

# 2

Two children were travelling, separately from different directions, to Iyot House, Iyot Lock, one hot afternoon in late June.

'Where am I to put them?' Mrs Mullen had asked, to whom children were anathema. 'Where will they sleep?'

Kestrel, the aunt, knew better than to make any suggestion, the housekeeper being certain to object and overrule.

'I wonder where seems best to you?' Images of the bedrooms flicked in a slide show through Aunt Kestrel's mind, each one seeming less suitable than the last – too dark, too large, too full of precious small objects. She had no experience of young children, though she was perfectly well disposed to the thought of having her great nephew and niece to stay, and had a vague idea that they were easily frightened of the dark or broke things. And were they to sleep in adjacent rooms or with a communicating door? On separate floors?

'The attics would suit best, in my view,' Mrs Mullen said.

Shadowy images chased across Kestrel's mind, troubling her enough to make her get up from her writing desk. 'I think we had better look. I can't remember when I was last up there.'

She went through the house, three flights of wide stairs, one of steep and narrow. Mrs Mullen did not trouble to follow, knowing it would all be decided satisfactorily.

The summer wind beat at the small latched windows but daylight changed its nature, making it seem a soft wind, and benign. The floorboards were dusty. Kestrel opened a cupboard set deep into the wall. The shelves were lined with newspaper and smelled of nothing worse than mothballs and old fluff. One of the rooms was completely empty, the second contained only a cracked leather trunk, but the two rooms next to one another, in the middle of the row, had furniture – an iron bed in each, a chest of drawers, a mirror. One had a wicker chair, one a musty velvet stool. And cupboards, more cupboards. She had lived here for over forty years and remembered a time when the attic rooms had been for maids. Now, there was Mrs Mullen, who had the basement, and a woman who came on a bicycle from a village on the other side of the fen.

The rooms could be made right, she thought, though vague as to exactly what children might need to make them so. Curtains? Rugs? Toys?

Well, linen at least.

'The attics,' she said, coming down from them, 'will do nicely.'


Kestrel Dickinson had been an only child for fourteen years before two sisters were born, Dora first and then Violet. Dora was plain and brown-eyed with brown straight hair and placid under the spotlight of everyone's attention. Their mother tried to conceal her disappointment, firstly that Dora was not a boy and secondly that she was not beautiful, though her love for both girls was never in doubt. Violet was born two years and two days after Dora and grew into a pert and extremely pretty child, with blonde bubble curls and intensely blue eyes, and was adored. She smiled, lisped, talked early, looked beautiful in frills, never got her clothes dirty, and laughed with delight at everyone who looked in her direction.

From the first Dora hated her and Violet learned quickly to meet like with like. As they grew into children and then young women, they quarrelled and despised one another. From the beginning the root of it all was Dora's jealousy, but Violet, who had had her head turned early, quickly turned proud, self-absorbed and boastful. In her turn, Dora behaved with pettiness and spite. Their feud became life-long. Violet married when she was eighteen, and again, at twenty-five and thirty-three. After that she had a succession of lovers but did not bother to marry them. When she was forty-two, she had her first and only child, Leonora, by a rich man called Philip van Vorst, before she embarked on eight years of restless travel, from Kenya to Paris, Peking to Los Angeles, Las Vegas to Hong Kong. Her daughter travelled with her, growing quickly used both to their nomadic life, a succession of substitute fathers, hotels, money and, like her mother, being pretty, spoilt, admired and both lonely and dissatisfied.

Violet rarely returned home, but whenever she did, she and Dora picked up their animosity where it had been left, always finding fresh things about which to quarrel. Violet's frivolous, amoral, butterfly nature infuriated her sister. She knew she behaved better, led a more wholesome life, but never managed to feel that these counted for anything when her sister arrived home showering presents out of her suitcases. The adoration she had always received shone out again from parents, servants, friends, everything that had been complained of was set aside. Dora, plain and brown, simmered in corners and, long into adult life, plotted obscure revenge. Violet had had three husbands, innumerable lovers – usually handsome, always rich – and a daughter with enviable looks. Dora had had one rather anonymous suitor who had never confessed any feelings for her and who had eventually faded from her life over a period of several months, while she remained waiting in hope.

By this time, Kestrel was long married and living at Iyot House, though she did not have children of her own and had detached herself from her feuding sisters, but had never stopped feeling guilt that she had not somehow succeeded in uniting them.

And then, in the flurry of less than three months, Dora had met and married George Cayley, a local widower almost thirty years her senior. A year later she had produced her small, frail son, Edward. Two years later both she and George were dead.

Kestrel inherited Iyot House from her own husband after a short marriage. At first she had disliked it and the expanse of dun-coloured fens, their watery aspect and huge oppressive skies, the isolation and lack of friends, the oddness of the villagers. In time, though, she grew used to it and found some sort of spirit half-hidden there. She had people to stay in the spring and summer and for the rest of the year was happy with her own company and her painstaking work as a botanical illustrator.

From Violet there came the occasional, erratic postcard which rarely mentioned her daughter Leonora but she heard nothing of her orphaned nephew until a letter had come asking if he might spend the summer at Iyot House. In some desperation she wrote to Violet.

'They are cousins after all and he will need a companion.'

It was settled.

# 3

'EDWARD CAYLEY,' he wrote in the steamed-up train window. 'Edward Laurence Cayley.' Then rubbed it out with his sleeve.

He had been driven from the house by his half-brother's business chauffeur and hurried across the concourse of Liverpool Street as if he must be bundled out of sight as quickly as possible. The driver carried his case; he carried a small hold-all. The station smelled of smoke, which tasted on his tongue and caught the back of his throat. His hold-all and suitcase had labels tied on with his name and the station to which he was travelling. He was put in charge of the guard, inspected, turned round, and then put into the van.

'Two hours.' The guard had several missing teeth and the rest were brown.

After that, there was nothing. No one looked at or

spoke to him, he had nothing to eat or drink. The train steamed on. He saw cows and churches, fields and houses, dykes and people on bicycles. He did not think and he did not feel, he simply accepted, having learned that accepting was the best and safest way.

He was neither happy nor unhappy: he was a frozen child, as he had been since he had arrived at the house of a half-brother who neither loved nor wanted him but who, with his wife, had looked after him dutifully, without fault or favour.

He was a pale, fair, thin boy, small for his age but fit and wiry now and with a sensitive and intelligent face. He was liked. It was taken for granted that he would find his way easily in life, that excuses would never need to be made for him.

But, looking out at the cows and sheep and churches and dykes and people on bicycles, he was unaware of any of this. He wrapped himself in a bubble of unknowing.

Leonora van Vorst travelled alone from Geneva the same day, with her name on a badge pinned to her coat and a brown suitcase covered in shipping line labels, thrown from porter to porter and, finally, to the driver of a hire car which was to take her from Dover to Iyot Lock. To anyone watching her follow the last porter with her case on his shoulder and her round overnight bag in his left hand, across the dock from the boat, she looked small, solemn and lost, but within herself, she was tall, confident and superior. She had money inside her glove for the last tip. The driver loaded her cases and pinched her cheek, feeling sorry for what he thought of as 'the little mite'. Leonora frowned and climbed into the back of the car without speaking. She was self-possessed, calm, haughty, and without any sense that there was such a thing as love, or vulnerability.

The car sped east and after only a few miles she began to feel sick, but fearing to mention it, and seem weak, she closed her eyes and imagined a sheet of smooth black paper, as her mother had once taught her, and eventually the nausea faded and she slept. Through the rear mirror the driver saw a white-faced child with a halo of red hair spread behind her on the back of the seat, lips pinched together and an expression he could not exactly make out, partly of detachment, partly of something like defiance.

# 4

'How do you do?' The boy put out his hand, Aunt . . .' But his voice wavered on the 'Kestrel.'

'Lord, I'm not your aunt. You'd better come in.' Mrs Mullen looked down at the boy's bags, both small. The taxi had already turned and started down the long straight road twelve miles back to the station.

'Well, pick them up.' She had no intention of waiting on two children.

'Oh. Yes.'

She did not know how a boy of eight should look but Edward Cayley seemed thin, his knee-caps protruding awkwardly from bony little legs. His hair was freshly cut, too short, leaving a fringe of bristle on his neck.

'Put them down there.'

'Yes.'

They stood in the dimness of the hall staring at one

another in silence for a full minute, Mrs Mullen struck by an unfamiliar sympathy for a child who was not like the few children she had known, who had been sturdy, loud, greedy, grubby and disrespectful. That was how village children were. Edward Cayley was the opposite of all those things and though she did not yet know about his appetite, no boy so thin, and pale as a peeled willow, could surely be a big eater.

Edward looked at Mrs Mullen, and then at his own feet, knowing that staring round a strange house was impolite. He could think of nothing to say, though he wondered who the woman was and where his Aunt Kestrel was, while knowing that the behaviour of adults was generally inexplicable.

The house smelled strange, half of living, breathing smells, half of age and damp.

'Wait there.'

'Yes.'

The woman disappeared into the dimness and a door bumped softly shut. He waited. All he knew was that Aunt Kestrel was related to the dead mother he did not remember and that he was to stay with her at Iyot for some weeks of this summer. He supposed that was enough.

In her dressing room, Kestrel adjusted her necklace, wondered if she should change it for another, put up her hands to the clasp and froze. The boy was here, and she was anxious. She had seen him once, as a baby of a month old, she did not know what he would be like and she was unused to children, but she was not innately hostile to them like Mrs Mullen. She wanted to make the boy comfortable, for him to talk to her, find entertainment, not be homesick or bored and now that he was here, her nerve failed her. But at least he would not be lonely.

The house was silent. Mrs Mullen had announced Edward's arrival and then disappeared. Aunt Kestrel, as she must now think of herself, replaced the necklace and went downstairs.

They had lunch in the dining room, he and the aunt, and he sat quiet, pale and watchful, eating everything he was offered quite slowly, made nervous by the room itself, with its heavy red curtains held back by brass rods, and large portraits of men with horses and dogs and women with hats and distant children.

'Are you enjoying your lunch? Is there anything else you would like?' He sensed with surprise that his aunt was as nervous as he was, and far more anxious to please. His own wish was more negative – not to annoy anyone, not to provoke irritation, not to be chastised, not to break anything. He had been warned so many

times about the breaking of objects, of china and orna-
ments and even windows, that he was in a state of
suspended terror, passing by the dresser with its huge
dishes, small tables with glass paperweights and gilded
figurines.

'Is your drink too strong?'

'It's very nice, thank you.'

It was lemon squash diluted so much that the water
was barely tinted.

'Do you like lamb chop?'

'Yes, thank you.'

'And how was your train journey? Were you prop-
erly looked after?'

'Yes, thank you. I travelled in the guard's van with
the guard.'

'Quite right. But was that uncomfortable?'

It had been. He had been forced to sit on someone's
leather trunk, next to cardboard boxes of live chicks
which chirped and rustled about and then went still,
until they were put out onto a station platform somewhere. But the guard had shared a chocolate bar with
him and told him stories about famous railway mur-
ders and ghosts in tunnels.

'It was very nice, thank you.'

He looked up from his plate at Aunt Kestrel just as
she looked straight at him. They took one another in.

She looked old to him, with a tweedy skirt and a buttoned blouse, and several rings on her left hand, but her face was soft and not at all unkind.

To her, the boy was alarmingly like his mother in profile, with the same long straight nose and small mouth, but his full face was like no one she recognised. He was nervous, polite and private, his true thoughts and feelings all his own and kept hidden. His manner deterred any questions other than those about the food and drink and his journey.

'Your cousin Leonora will come tomorrow. Have you met her before?'

He shook his head, his mouth full of pears and custard.

'I thought not. She is your Aunt Violet's only child – Violet and your mother were sisters and . . . well, and I was sister to them both, of course. But older. Much older.'

He said nothing.

'So you are quite close in age. I hope you'll get on.'

He did not know what to say, having no sense at all of what it might be like to spend a whole summer with a girl cousin he had never seen.

'What would you like to do now? Do you have a rest after lunch? I'm afraid I'm not used to – to what children . . . boys . . . do. Have you brought any books to read or do you play with . . . Or you could go into the garden.'

He followed her into the hall. 'But I expect you'd like to see your room and so on now.'

'Thank you.'

Mrs Mullen appeared from behind a baize-covered door.

'I'll take him up then shall I?'

He did not want her to but could not have said and they all three stood about uncertainly for a moment.

'Well, perhaps I should . . . you carry on with the dining room, Mrs Mullen.'

He noted the name.

'Pick those up then,' Mrs Mullen said, pointing to his bags, the small one and the very small.

'Yes.'

Edward picked them up and followed his aunt to the stairs.

# 5

'AT WHAT time should you go up?'

Edward looked up from the solitaire board. Aunt Kestrel had unlocked a cupboard in the drawing room, whose blinds were pulled down all day as well as at night, and found the solitaire, a shove ha'penny board and a pile of jigsaw puzzles which he had taken up to the attics. He examined the glass marbles again. They were wonderful colours, deep sea green, brilliant blue, blood red, and clear glass enclosing swirls of misty grey. The board was carved out of rosewood with green velvet covering the underside.

'Do you have something to eat first, or . . .'

'I have milk and two biscuits at seven and then I go to bed.'

'Of course, these are the holidays; I daresay rules should be stretched. When would you like to go up?'

The idea that he could choose his own time, that routine was not made of iron but could be broken, was not only new but alarming.

'I am quite tired,' he said, moving a blue marble over a clear glass one, to leave only seven on the board. His aunt had shown him how to play and as it had been raining, he had done so, sitting beside the window, for most of the afternoon. Seven was the smallest number he had got down to without being unable to move again.

'You have had a rather dull day.'

'It has been very nice, thank you.'

Kestrel was taken aback again by the opaque politeness of the child.

'You will have more fun when Leonora arrives. And this miserable rain. We don't get a lot of rain at Iyot but we do get wind. Wind and skies.'

He thought everyone had sky, or skies, but perhaps this was not the case. He didn't ask.

'Five!' he said under his breath, removing another blue.

'Excellent.'

Mrs Mullen brought in a small glass of milk and two garibaldi biscuits on a lacquer tray.

'Thank you very much,' he said, stopping in the doorway. 'I have had a very nice day.'

His earnest, unformed face stayed with Kestrel for

a long time after he had gone. He was her own flesh and blood, he was part of her. She did not know him, as she had not known Dora after she had grown up and married, and yet she felt connected to him and his words touched her deeply, his vulnerability impressed itself on her so that she felt suddenly afraid on his behalf and had an urge to protect him. But he had gone, his footsteps mounting the stairs carefully until they went away to the fourth flight and the attics.

Once he was there, Edward put his milk and the hated garibaldi biscuits carefully on the table beside his bed, and went to look out of the window. It was very high. The sky was huge and full of sagging leaden clouds, making the night seem closer than it was by the clock. Ragged jackdaws whirled about on the wind like scraps of torn burned paper. He could see the church tower, the churchyard, the road, and the flat acres of fen with deep dykes criss-crossing them. A small stone bridge. A brick cottage beside a lock, though he did not yet know that was what it was called.

He drank the milk in small sips and wondered what he could do with the biscuits that he could not have swallowed any more than he could have swallowed a live spider. In the end, he opened the cupboard in the wall. It was completely empty. He broke off a corner of the biscuit and crumbled it onto the plate, and climbed up and put the rest far back on the highest shelf he could reach. Perhaps mice would find it. He was not afraid of mice.

And then, as he turned round, he felt something strange, like a rustle of chill across his face, or someone blowing towards him. It was soundless but something in the cupboard caught his eye and he thought that the paper lining the shelves had lifted slightly, as if the movement of air had caught that too.

He went back to the window but it was closed tightly, and the latch was across. It was the same with the window on the other side. He touched the door but it was closed firmly and it did not move. The room was still again.

Five minutes later, he was in bed, lying flat on his back with the sheet just below his chin, both hands holding it. The wind had got up now. The windows rattled, the sound round the rooftop above him grew louder and then wild, as the gale came roaring across the fen to hit the old house and beat it about the head.

Edward did not remember such a wind but it was outside and could not get in, and so he was not in the least afraid, any more than he was afraid of the sound of rain, or the rattle of hail on a pane. He had left the wall cupboard slightly open but the lining paper did not lift, and there was no chill breeze across his face. This was just weather. This was different.

He went to sleep rocked by the storm, and it howled through his dreams and made him turn over and over in the narrow bed, and in her own room, Kestrel lay troubled by it not for herself, well used to it as she was, but for the boy. At one point when the gale was at its height she almost got up and went to him, but surely, if he were alarmed he would call out, and she felt shy of indicating her feelings or of transmitting alarm. High winds were part of the warp and weft of the place and the old house absorbed them without complaint.

He would get used to them, and when Violet's child came tomorrow, so would she, whatever she was like.

A vision of her sister came into Kestrel's mind as she fell asleep, of the bubble curls and pretty mouth and the coquettish charm she had been mistress of at birth. Leonora. Leonora van Vorst. What sort of a child would Leonora be?

# 6

H E WAS sitting on the edge of his bed reading and as he still did not find reading easy, although he loved what he discovered in a book when he found the key to it, he had to concentrate hard and so he did not hear the footsteps on the last flights of uncarpeted stairs or their voices. He read on and one set of footsteps went away again and it was quiet, late afternoon. It had stopped raining, the wind had dropped and there was an uncertain sun on the watery fens.

And then he was aware of her, standing just inside the doorway, and looked up with a start.

'You seem to be very easily frightened,' she said.

Edward stared at the girl. She had dark red hair, long and standing out from her head as if she had an electric shock running through her, and dark blue eyes in a china white face.

'I'm not frightened at all.'

She smiled a small superior smile and came right into the room to stand a yard or two away from him.

He slid off the bed, remembering manners he had been taught almost from the cradle, and put out his hand.

'I am Edward Cayley,' he said. 'I suppose you're my cousin Leonora.'

She looked at the hand but did not take it.

'How do you do?'

She smiled again, then turned abruptly and went to the window.

'This is a dreadful place,' she said. 'What are we supposed to do?'

'It isn't actually terrible. It is quiet though.'

'Who is that woman?'

'Our aunt. Aunt Kestrel.'

Leonora tossed her hair. 'The other one, with the sour face.'

He smiled. 'Mrs Mullen.'

'She doesn't like us.'

'Doesn't she?'

'Don't be stupid, can't you tell? But what does it matter?' She looked round his room, summing its contents up quickly, then sat down on the bed.

'Where have you come from?' He opened his mouth to say 'London' but she carried on without waiting to hear. 'I came from Geneva this time,' she said, 'but before that from Hong Kong and before that from Rome. Not that way round.'

'How did you do that?'

'Well on a ship and a train, of course. I might have flown but it seemed better.'

'Not on your own.'

'Of course on my own, why not? Did you have to have someone to bring you, like an escort.'

'I came in charge of the guard.'

'Oh yes, I've done that. I came in charge of stewards and so on.' She bounced off the bed. 'Your mother's dead.'

'I know.'

'What did she die of?'

'I'm not sure. No one has ever said.'

'Goodness. My mother's alive, so is my father, but somewhere else. At the moment my stepfather is called Claude. I hope he stays, I quite like Claude, but, of course, he won't, they never do for long.'

He caught sight of her face then and it was strange and sad and distant.

'We could go out into the garden.'

'Why? Is it interesting? I don't expect so. Gardens aren't usually.'

'Our aunt found some jigsaw puzzles.'

Leonora was at the window.

'Shall I get them out?'

'I don't want to do one but you can.'

'No, it's all right. How long did it take you to get here?'

'Two days. I slept on the boat train.'

'Were you sick?'

He had gone to stand beside her at the window and he saw that he had made her angry.

'I am never sick. I am an excellent sailor. I suppose you're sick.

'Anyway, it doesn't matter. Some people are, some aren't and you can't die of being sick.'

Her eyes seemed to darken and the centres to grow smaller. 'Where do you think people go when they die?'

Edward hesitated. He did not know how to behave towards her, whether she wanted to be friendly or hostile, if she was worried about something or about nothing.

'They go to heaven. Or . . . to God.'

'Or to hell.'

'I'm not sure.'

'Hell isn't fire you know.'

'Isn't it?'

'Oh no. Hell is a curse. You're forced to wander this world and you can never escape.'

'That sounds all right. It's what – you wander this world. You've wandered to all those places.'

He could sense something in her that needed reassurance and could not ask for it. He did not know, because he was too young and had never before encountered it, that what he sensed in Leonora was pride. Later, he was to understand, though still without having a word for it.

'Do you remember your mother?'

'No. Aunt Kestrel does but she didn't want to talk about her.'

'What, because it might upset you? How could you be upset about a mother you don't remember?'

'No. I think it – it might have upset her.'

'Oh.'

That was something else he would come to know well, the tone of her voice that signified boredom.

'Tomorrow we'll play a trick on that woman,' she said next. 'I'll think of something she won't like at all.' She sounded so full of a sort of evil glee at the idea that she alarmed him.

'I don't think we ought to do that.'

Leonora turned on him in scorn. 'Why? Do you want to be her favourite and have her pet you?'

He flushed. 'No. I just think it would be a bad thing to do. And mean.'

'Of course it would be a bad thing to do. And mean. How silly you are.'

'I don't think she's very nice but perhaps it's because

45

she hasn't any children of her own or doesn't know any.'

'Aunt Kestrel hasn't any children but she doesn't hate us.'

'I don't think Mrs Mullen would hate us.'

'Of course she hates us. And I am going now to think about what trick to play.'

'Where are you going?'

But she had already gone. She came and went so silently and completely that he wondered if she did not move at all but simply knew how to just appear and disappear.

He did not see her again until the bell rang for supper and then, just as he was going across the hall, she was there, when she had not been there a second before.

From now on, he determined to watch her.

'Have you thought?'

But Leonora stared at him blankly across the table.

'I wish the weather would improve,' Aunt Kestrel said, slicing a tea-cake and buttering half for each of them. 'You would find so many good things to do out of doors.'

'What things?'

Aunt Kestrel looked like someone caught out in a lie. That is how Leonora makes me feel, Edward realised, as if she can see through me to my soul and know

46

what I am thinking and if I am telling the truth, or trying to bluff my way out of something.

She had not yet been here for a whole day and already the mood of the house had been changed entirely.

'My mother is said to be the most beautiful woman who has ever lived,' Leonora said now. 'Did you know that?'

'How ridiculous,' Aunt Kestrel said, spluttering out some little droplets of tea. 'Of course she is not. Violet was a pretty little girl and grew up to be a pretty woman, though she was helped by clothes and having people to bring out the best in her.'

'What people?'

'Oh, hairdressers and . . . you know, those people. But as to being the most beautiful woman who ever lived . . . besides, who could know?'

'It was written in a magazine of fashion.' Leonora's face had changed as a blush of annoyance rose through the paleness and her eyes darkened. 'It was written under her photograph so it would have to be true. Of course it is true. She is very, very beautiful. She is.' Edward watched in horror as Leonora stood up and picked up a small silver cake fork. 'She is, she is, she is.' As she said it, she stabbed the fork down into the cloth and through to the table, one hard stab for each word. Aunt Kestrel's mouth was half open, her arm slightly outstretched as if she meant to stop the dreadful stabbing, but was unable to make any movement.

'And no one is allowed to say it is not true.'

She dropped the fork on the floor and it spun away from her, and then she was gone, the skirt of her blue cotton frock seeming to flick out behind her and then disappear as she disappeared. The door closed slowly of its own accord. Edward sat, wishing that he was able to disappear too but forced to wait for Aunt Kestrel's anger to break over him and take whatever punishment there might be, for them both.

There was none. His aunt sat silent for a moment then said, 'I wonder if you can find out what is wrong, Edward?'

He sped to the door. 'She is like her mother,' she said as he went, but he thought that she was speaking to herself, not to him.

'She is too like her mother.'

# 7

H E DID not see Leonora and the door of her room was shut. He hesitated, listening. The wind had dropped. There was no sound from her and he opened his mouth to say her name, then did not, afraid that her anger was still raging and that she might turn it on him. He thought of the cake fork stabbing into the table.

The house no longer felt strange to him but he did not like it greatly and he was disappointed that his cousin seemed unlikely to become a friend. She was strange, if Iyot House and their Aunt Kestrel were not. She belonged with Mrs Mullen, he thought, turning on his left side. The last of the light was purple and pale blue in a long thread across the sky, seen through the window opposite his bed. It had not been like this before. Perhaps there would be sun tomorrow and they could explore the world outside. Perhaps things would improve, as in Edward's experience they often did. His school had improved, his eczema had improved, his dog had improved with age after being disobedient and running away all through puppy-hood.

He went to sleep optimistically.

There was moonlight and so he could see her when he woke very suddenly.

Leonora was standing in the doorway, her night-gown as white as her skin, her red hair standing out from her head. She was absolutely still, her eyes oddly blank and for several moments Edward thought that she was an apparition. Or a ghost. What was the difference?

'Hello?'

She didn't reply.

'Are you quite all right?'

She did not move. He saw that her feet were bare. Long pale feet. He did not know what to do.

And then she came further into the room, silently on the long pale feet, her hair glowing against the whiteness of her skin and long nightgown.

'Leonora?'

She had walked to the window and was looking out, washed by the moonlight.

Edward got up and went to stand beside her. At first

he did not touch her, hardly dared to look directly at her. He had the odd sense that if he did touch her she would feel cold.

'Are you still asleep?'

She turned her head and stared at him out of the blank unseeing eyes.

'You should go back to your own room now. You could hurt yourself.'

Stories of people walking out of windows and far from home across fields and into woods while they were deeply asleep came into his mind.

You should not try to wake a sleepwalker, the shock could kill them. You should not touch a sleepwalker, or they may stay that way and never wake again.

He began to panic when Leonora sat on the ledge and started to undo the window latch, and then he did reach out and touch her shoulder. She stopped but did not look at him.

'Come on. We're going back now.'

He nudged her gently and she got up and let him guide her out of his room and back to her own. He steered her to the bed, pulled back the covers and she climbed in obediently, and turned on her side. Her eyes closed. Edward spread the covers over her with care and watched her until he was sure she was fully asleep, then crept out.

# 8

'OH DO hurry up, hurry up . . .'

Aunt Kestrel came into the hall. 'If you are going out you need stout shoes. The grass is very wet.'

Leonora ignored her, hand on the front door.

Edward looked at his feet. Were the shoes 'stout'?

'Well, perhaps you'll be all right. Don't go too far.'

'Hurry up,' Leonora said again. The inner door opened and she went to the heavy outer one, which had a large iron key and a bolt and chain.

'Anyone would suppose ravening beasts and highwaymen would be wanting to burst in,' she said, laughing a small laugh.

Mrs Mullen was in the dark recesses of the hall watching, lips pinched together.

Aunt Kestrel sighed as she closed both doors. She was confused by the children, and bewildered.

Leonora was like Violet, which boded ill though perhaps not in quite the same way, who knew? Edward was simply opaque. Had they taken to one another? Were they settling?

She went into her sitting room with the morning paper.

Mrs Mullen did not ask the same questions because she had made up her mind from seeing both children, Edward, the little namby-pamby, too sweet-tongued to trust, and Leonora. She had looked into Leonora's eyes when she had first arrived, and seen the devil there and her judgment was made and snapped shut on the instant.

'Where are you going?' Edward watched his cousin going to the double gates. 'The garden is on this side.'

Leonora gave her usual short laugh. 'Who wants to go in a garden?'

She lifted the latch of a small gate within the gate and stepped through. He went after her because he thought he should look after her and persuade her to come back, but by the time he had clambered over the bottom strut she was walking fast down the road and a minute later, had crossed it and started up the path that led to the open fens.

'Leonora, we'd better not . . .'

She tossed her red hair and went on.

When he caught her up she was standing on the bank looking down into the river. It was inky and slick and ran quite slowly.

'Be careful.'

'Can you swim?'

'No, can you?'

'I wonder what you can do. Of course I can swim, one of my stepfathers taught me in . . . I think it was Italy.'

'How many have you had? Stepfathers?'

She did not answer, but moved away and followed a rivulet that led away from the main course deep into the fen. They looked back. Iyot House reared up, higher than the other huddled houses, dark behind its trees. The church rose like a small ship towards the west.

It was very still, not cold. The reeds stood like guardsmen.

'Where are we going?'

'Anywhere.'

But it was only a little further on when she stopped again. The rivulet had petered out and widened to form a pool, which reflected the sky, the clouds which were barely moving.

'There might be newts here,' Edward said.

'Are they like lizards?'

'I think so.'

'There are lizards everywhere in hot countries. On stones. On walls. They slither into the cracks. Are you afraid of things like that?'

'I've never seen one.'

She faced him, her eyes challenging, dark as sloes in her face.

'Are you afraid of hell? Or snakes or mad bulls or fire coming out of people's mouths?'

Edward laughed.

'You should be careful,' she said softly. 'Mind what you laugh at. See if there are any of your newt things in there.'

They bent over and, instinctively, Edward reached out to take her hand in case she went too near to the edge. Leonora snatched it away as if his own had burned her, making him almost lose his balance.

'Don't you ever dare to do that again.'

He wanted to weep with frustration at this girl who made him feel stupid, and so as not to show his face to her, he knelt down and stared into the water, trying hopelessly to see newts, or frogs – any living, moving creature.

'Oh. How strange.'

Leonora was pointing to the smooth, still surface of the water. At first, Edward could not see anything except the sky, which now had patches of blue behind the white clouds. He looked harder and saw what he thought was – must be – Leonora's face reflected in the water, and there was his own, wavery but recognisably him.

Leonora's red hair spread out in the water like weed, and the collar of her blue frock was clear, and a little of her long pale neck. But her face was not the same. Or rather, it was the same but . . .

'Oh,' he said.

'Who is it?' Leonora whispered.

He could not tell her. He could not say, because he did not really know, who he saw or what. He reached out his hand to her and she held it fast in her own, so tight that it seemed to hurt his bones.

'What is it? What can you see?'

She went on staring, still gripping his hand, but even when he bent down, Edward could only make out the blurred reflection of both their faces upside down. There was nothing behind them and you could not see below.

'You're hurting my hand.'

And then, she was scrabbling in the earth for small stones, and clods of turf, and then larger stones. She threw them into the water and then hurled the largest one and their images splintered and the water rocked and in a moment, stilled again and there they were, the boy Edward, the girl Leonora. Nothing else.

'I don't understand,' Edward said. But she had gone,

racing away from him along the path. He watched her, troubled, but he knew he ought not to let her be by herself, sensing that she was quixotic and unsafe, and followed her from a distance but always keeping her in sight as she ran in the direction of Iyot Church.

# 9

'WHAT DID you see?' Edward asked.

He had found her wandering round the side aisles looking at memorial tablets set into the walls and brasses into the floor, running her hand over the carved pew ends and the steps of the pulpit, lifting the hassocks off their hooks and dropping them onto the pews, going restlessly, pointlessly from one to the other.

She did not answer. He was worried, felt responsible.

'I think we should go now. Maybe we aren't allowed in here at all.'

Leonora came to his side, smiling. 'What do you think would happen to us?'

'We'd get into trouble.'

'Who from?'

'The parson.'

She shook her head. Her hair lifted and seemed to float out from her head, then settle back.

'God?'

'Or the devil.'

'Why would the devil care? It isn't his place.'

'Do you believe in them?'

'Of course I do,' Edward said. 'Look – that is God, in that window.'

'And there is the devil, at the bottom of that picture.' Her voice was scornful.

'No, that's a snake.'

'The devil is a serpent, which is what a snake is in the Bible. I know a lot about it.'

'I still think we should go.'

But before he could move, Leonora had taken hold of his hand again and was pressing her fingernails into the palm. She was staring at a large silver plate that stood on a dark wooden chest against the wall beside them.

'What's the matter? I think it's for collecting money. You know, when they go round.'

But she seemed not to hear him, only went on looking at the shining circle, her face pale as paper, eyes coal-dark.

He got up and went to the dish. His own face reflected shimmering in the surface though it was distorted and hard to make out.

'Don't look,' Leonora said. 'Move away from it, don't look.'

'Why? It isn't dangerous.'

He was about to bend right over and put his face very close to the silver, when Leonora leaped up, lifted the plate and hurled it away from her down the aisle. It crashed against the stone flags and then went rolling crazily until it spun and fell flat in a corner.

'Why did you do that?'

But she was gone again, out of the church, leaving the door wide open, and away down the path before jumping off between two high gravestones. The wind had got up again and was bending the tall uncut grasses and the branches of the yew.

This time, Edward did not race after her. He was tired of what he decided was some sort of game which she would not explain to him and in which he had no part, but he also thought that she was trying to frighten him and he was not going to allow it.

He came slowly out of the church and down the path to the gate. Then he looked round but could not see her. She had gone back to the house then. He would see her racing down the road.

As he put his hand on the gate, the heavy wooden door of the church banged loudly shut behind him in the wind.

Leonora was nowhere ahead. He turned, and then

60

caught a glimpse of her, low down behind the stone
wall among the gravestones. The wind caught the
edge of her blue frock and lifted it a little.

'Leonora . . .'

What he saw on her face when she glanced round
was a look so full of malice and evil, so twisted and
distorted with dislike and scorn and a sort of laughing
hatred, that he wanted to be the one to run, to get
away as fast as he could, back to what he now thought
of as the safety and shelter of Iyot House. But as long
as she looked at him, he could not move, his limbs, his
body, even his breath, seemed to be paralysed. He
could not even cry out or speak because his lungs and
his mouth felt full of heavy sand. Her look lasted for
hours, for years; he was struck dumb and motionless
for a lifetime, while Leonora held his gaze.

But he was just as suddenly free and light as air and
full of almost electric energy, and he ran.

The hands of the clock on the church tower had
not moved.

For the rest of that day and several days more they fell
under the spell of Bagatelle, after Aunt Kestrel had
unearthed the old set and taught the game to them.

'And if you grow tired of that, here are the cards. I will
teach you Piquet.'

But they did not grow tired. The weather changed and became hot, with clear, blue skies that paled to white on the horizon and a baking sun. The streams dried, the pond was lower, the river ran sluggishly. The air smelled of heat, heat seemed to fill their mouths and scratch at their eyes. They went into the garden under the shade of a huge copper beech and set the Bagatelle board out on an old table. Mrs Mullen brought a jug of lukewarm lemon barley and the despised garibaldi biscuits and they played game after game, mainly in silence. At first, Leonora won. She was quicker and slyer and saw her chances. Edward was cautious and steady. At home he played chess with his half-brother.

There was a small fish pond over which dragonflies hovered, their blue sheen catching the sun, and the flower beds were seething with bees.

'At last,' Aunt Kestrel said, as Mrs Mullen brought in her coffee. 'They have settled down together perfectly well.'

Mrs Mullen went to the window and saw the table, the game, the boy and girl bent over the board, one fair head, one brilliant red. She mistrusted the girl and thought the boy a namby-pamby. Either way, having children to stay in the house had not altered her opinion, except to harden it against them.

'I agree with you that Leonora behaved very badly,

but we have to forgive her. It is all so strange and odd for them. Don't bear a grudge, Mrs Mullen.'

After the housekeeper had gone out of the room, Kestrel sat thinking about her, wondering why she was so very hostile, so clearly unable to warm to either child in any way, so readily seeing the bad and fearing worse. She knew little of her background and former life, other than that she had no children and her husband worked as a bargeman. Why she was so embittered she could not fathom.

The heat continued until the air grew stale and every morning was more oppressive than the last. The sun filmed over with a haze and midges jazzed above the waterways.

'Time we had a storm,' Aunt Kestrel said over supper at the beginning of the third week of heat.

Edward looked apprehensive. Leonora, on the other side of the table, saw his face and frowned. The previous day he had beaten her three times at Bagatelle and now she played with an angry concentration, determined to win and breathless with silent fury when, time after time, she did not.

The heat formed a heavy cloud that hung low over the garden, obscuring any sun. Edward's skin itched inside his clothes.

'Let's stop.'

'No. I have to win first.'

'You can win another time. It's too hot.'

'Stupid. I said I want to win first, then we can stop.'

'You might not win for another ten games. I'm going to read indoors by the window.'

In a single flash of movement, Leonora stood up, overturned the Bagatelle board, sending it flying onto the grass and scattering its pieces, and then she screamed, a terrible, violent scream, so loud that Edward ran from her and from the awful sound of it, across the garden, up the steps and into the house, slamming the heavy door behind him.

Mrs Mullen was in the shadows of the hall, making him start.

'I said everything would be turned upside down and we would have nothing but upset and disturbance, but never did I expect what came here.'

Edward dared not move.

'Listen to it.'

She was still screaming without apparently needing to pause for breath.

'It will turn you as well. In the end, there'll be not a pin to put between you. Can you not feel it?'

'Feel it?' Edward could scarcely hear his own voice speaking into the dark hall.

'What possesses her? Can you not feel it creeping over you too? No child could come within sight of her and not be turned.' She came out of the shadows and went smartly to the door, turned the key and slid the bolt.

'What are you doing?'

'Shutting the door against her,' Mrs Mullen said. 'Now you get off upstairs out of the sight and sound of her while you've a chance.'

'But how will she get in?'

'Maybe she won't and that would be no bad thing.' She left him.

For several minutes, Edward stood wondering what he should do but in the end, after listening for any sound of Mrs Mullen's return, he went to the drawing room, in which they had only been allowed to step once and where there were French windows opening onto the side terrace and the wide stone steps to the garden below. The air was sultry, the sky gathering into a yellowish mass like a boil over the house. He went to where they had been sitting earlier. The Bagatelle was still scattered over the grass and the table upturned.

'Ah, she's sent the good little boy to tidy up.' He spun round. Leonora had appeared from nowhere and was standing a few yards from him.

'I came to find you. She locked the door to keep you out but she shouldn't have done that. I think there is going to be a storm.'

'Are you frightened of storms?'

'No. But you might have been.'

Leonora laughed the dry little laugh 'I'm not afraid of anything at all.'

'You were frightened of something. You were frightened of something down in the water.'

She lunged forward, grabbed his arm and bent it backwards so that he cried out. 'You must never ever say that again and I didn't see anything and I was not afraid. I am never afraid. Say it. "Leonora is never afraid."' She twisted his arm a little further back.

'Leonora is never afraid let go of my arm you're hurting.'

'Manners, little boy. "Please."'

'Please.'

She almost tossed his arm away from her, turned and went round to the side of the house. Edward followed her, angry that he had bothered to worry about her and feel worried enough to come and find her.

She ran up the steps, and through the French windows which he had left ajar, but as he came up behind her, shut them quickly and turned the key. Then she stood, her face close to the glass, looking out at him, smiling.

## 10

Edward woke when his room flared white and then for a split second, vivid blue. The thunder came almost simultaneously, seeming to crack the attic roof open like an axe splitting a log. He sat up watching it through the curtainless window for a while, until hail spattered so fiercely onto the glass that sudden light and sudden dark were all he could see. He lay down and listened. He had been two or three years old when his half-brother had taken him on a boat and out to sea; they had huddled together in the small cabin as a storm flared and crashed all round them. His brother had been bright-eyed with excitement and Edward had sensed that this was something to revel in, knowing no danger, only the drama and heightened atmosphere. He had loved storms from

67

then, though there had never been one so momentous. Now, this was almost as good, vast and overpowering across the fens and around Iyot House.

The lightning flickered vividly across the sky again and in the flash, he saw Leonora standing in the doorway of his room, her eyes wide, face stark white.

Edward sat up. 'It's amazing! I love storms.'

She went to his window. 'Yes.' She spoke in a whisper, as if she were afraid speaking aloud might change it.

Edward got up and stood beside her.

'You should see the storms in the East. A storm across the water in Hong Kong. A storm over the mountains. They race through your blood, such storms.'

He understood her at once and for the first time they shared something completely, bound up together in the excitement and pleasure of the storm, so that he clasped hold of her hand when a thunderclap made the house shake and the walls of the attics shudder and her nails dug into his palm at a blue-green zigzag of lightning.

'I thought you would be crying,' Leonora said, glancing at him sideways.

'Oh no, oh no!'

'We could go out.'

'Don't be silly, it's like a monsoon, we'd be soaked in a minute.'

'Have you been in a monsoon? I have. The earth steams and you could boil a pan of water on the ground. It brings down whole trees.'

'I want to go there.'

They were linked in a passion to soar from this storm to that one.

'My mother is there now,' Leonora said.

'Where? In a monsoon?'

'In India, I think. Or Burma. Or perhaps she is back in Hong Kong. They move about so.'

He was unsure whether to be envious or sorry for her.

'When will she come back for you?'

Leonora shrugged and flicked her hair about her shoulders. The storm was receding, the lightning moving away to the east and the sea, the rain easing to a steady, dull downpour.

'I hope she'll come before too long,' Edward said. 'You must miss her very much.'

'I don't,' Leonora said, 'and I don't.' And sailed out of the room on her bare and silent feet.

The next morning, the parcels began to arrive. There were two, one very large, one small, and after that, as the post from abroad caught up, one or two almost every day. Leonora took them upstairs, ignoring the remarks made by Mrs Mullen about spoilt children and the concern of Aunt Kestrel that perhaps some should be put away until later.

'They are my parcels,' she said, dragging a heavy one behind her, refusing help.

'But you,' she said to Edward, 'may look if you like.'

Most of the parcels contained clothes, few of which fitted, dresses made of bright silk embroidered with gold thread and decorated with little mirrors, trailing fine scarves and long skirts with several floating panels. Leonora glanced at each one, held it up to herself, then tossed it away, to fall on the floor or her bed. Once or twice she put on a scarf and twirled round in it and kept it on. There were silver boxes and carved wooden animals, brass bells and on one day a huge box of pale green and pink Turkish delight that smelled of scent and sent a puff of white sugar into the air when she lifted the wooden lid. They ate several pieces, one small, sticky bite at a time, and the intense sweetness set their teeth on edge.

'My mother never sends what I really want. She just doesn't.'

'But the sweets are nice. What do you really want?'
'One thing.'
'What thing?'

'And she knows and she never sends it.'

'When is your birthday?'

'August the tenth; I am a Leo.'

'That is quite soon. So I think she is going to send it for then.'

Leonora ripped open the thin brown paper on her last parcel. It contained a black satin cushion covered in gold and silver beads.

'How horrible, horrible, *horrible*.' The cushion bumped against the far wall and fell.

Edward wiped the sugar powder off his mouth. 'What is it that you do really want?'

'A doll,' Leonora said. 'You would think she could easily send me a doll but she never, never, never does. I hate my mother.'

'No, you should never say that.'

'Why? I do.'

'No.'

'Why?'

'Because – you just shouldn't.'

'You don't know anything about it. You don't know anything about mothers because you haven't got one.'

'I know,' Edward said. 'But I did once have one.'

'If she sent me what I wanted I would be able to love her.'

He wondered if that could be true, that someone made you love them by giving you what you wanted, or, that you would not love them until they did. It was confusing.

'I think that she will send you a doll. I think you will get it on your birthday.'

But the birthday came and she did not.

Aunt Kestrel gave her an ivory carved chess set in a wooden casket, a set of hairbrushes and a jar of sweets, which she had handed to Edward the night before, to hand over as from himself. Leonora's face had been pinched and sallow and when she had taken her things upstairs, with the handkerchief embroidered with her initial from Mrs Mullen, Edward had gone in to their aunt's sitting room.

'She doesn't mean to be ungrateful.'

'No. It is hard to know what to give but I thought you might teach her chess as you are so fond of it.' The Bagatelle board had been damaged beyond repair by being left outside in the storm.

'Yes. It is her mother.'

Aunt Kestrel sighed.

'She sends her so many parcels with nice things but never what she really wants.'

'The trouble is, Violet barely knows her own child and always had more interest in herself than anyone else. You will please never repeat that, Edward.'

'No.'

He explained about the doll.

'It seems an obvious thing to send. But I am going to London next week. If Violet has not had the sense to send a doll, I must find one.'

# I I

ANOTHER STORM was building for the whole day Aunt Kestrel was away. The fen was dun green with the river like an oil slick where it ran deep between its banks. Edward watched the lock keeper pace slowly along, peering into the water, cross the bridge, then walk back. The thunder rumbled round the edges of the sky.

Leonora was sullen and silent, not wanting to learn chess, not wanting to have him anywhere near her. In the end, he found a book about adventures in the diamond mines of South Africa, and read it sitting on the windowsill. Mrs Mullen rang them down for lunch, which was cold beef, cold potatoes and hard boiled eggs, with custard to follow, and they ate it silently in the dining room as the rain began to teem down the windows.

Mrs Mullen did not come near to them for the rest

of the day. She rang the supper bell, told them they must be in bed by eight o'clock, and disappeared behind her door.

Eight came and the attics were pitch dark. The storm had fizzled out but the rain was so loud they could not hear themselves speak, but did a jigsaw in silence. Leonora was bored and lost interest. Edward went to bed and read his book. He was not unhappy at Iyot House. He was a boy of equable temperament and no strong passions, who was never seriously unhappy anywhere, but tonight, he wished strongly that he could be at home in his own London bed. How long he and Leonora were staying here no one had said.

He usually slept deeply and dreamed little, but tonight, he fell into a restless, uncomfortable doze, skidding along the surface of strange dreams and hearing sounds that half woke him. He had an odd sense that something was about to happen, as if Iyot House and everyone in it were a bubbling pan about to boil over and hiss out onto a stove. In the middle of the night, he woke yet again, to the sound of crying, but it was not coming from his cousin's room, it came from somewhere near at hand and the crying was of a baby not a girl like Leonora.

He sat up. Everything was still. There was very little wind but clouds slid in front of a full moon now and again.

Nothing stirred. No one cried.

He lay down again but the strange sensation of foreboding did not leave him, even in sleep.

And then, a different sort of crying woke him, and this time he recognised it.

He went to Leonora. She had her head half underneath her pillow, which lifted and fell occasionally.

'It's all right.'

He pretended not to hear her when she told him to go away. It had been a miserable birthday and he was sorry for her.

'I want you to tell me something.'

She flung her pillow off her face. 'I said to . . .'

'I know but I'm not going to. I want you to tell me.'

Leonora turned her back on him.

'What kind of doll would you like best? I want you to tell me what it would look like, tell me everything.'

'Why? You can't get it for me so why would I tell you?'

'I can't get it for you but I can do something else.'

Silence. Then she sat up and pushed her hair out of her eyes. Edward was careful not to stare at her.

'I've got paper and some pencils and paints and I can draw it for you.'

She made a scornful sound in her throat.

'Isn't it better than no doll? And Aunt Kestrel is bringing you one.'

'She wouldn't find anything like this.'

'But she will find something nice.'

She described the doll she wanted very well, so that Edward could draw and then paint it with the greatest care. It was an Indian royal bride, with elaborate clothes and jewels and braiding in her hair, which Leonora knew in every tiny detail, every colour and shading and texture.

'Have you wanted one like it for a very long time?'

'Since I was about two or three. It is the only thing I ever ever wanted and my mother knows that and she has never got it for me.'

'Perhaps she tried hard and couldn't. Perhaps there has never been one like it in any shop.'

'Of course there hasn't, she should have had it made for me.'

He went on painting the doll, wondering as he did so why Leonora did not know that it was impolite to demand and want and order presents.

'I think it's finished but I shall put it here to dry.' He was afraid to wait until she had looked at it and went back quietly to bed, and slept at once.

The following morning, he went by himself out to the garden early, before breakfast. Leonora did not follow him for a long time but eventually she came, carrying the picture he had painted.

'I'm sorry it's not a doll,' Edward said.

'Yes. But there will be a doll. Just exactly like this. I know there will.'

She put the painting down on the grass. She had not thanked him for it and he was not very surprised that she left it there when they had to run in from the heavy rain.

She asked a hundred times when Aunt Kestrel would be back from London. Mrs Mullen said, 'When she's ready.' Edward said cautiously that it might be after they were asleep.

'I won't go to sleep until I see the doll.'

She did not. It was after eleven o'clock when she woke Edward to say that she had heard the station taxi.

'Get up, get up, I'm going downstairs.'

Her eyes were wild with excitement and she had two small spots of colour burning in the pale of her face. She raced down the stairs so fast he was afraid she would trip but her feet seemed not to touch the ground. She burst into Aunt Kestrel's sitting room but then some sense of how to behave touched her enough to make her stop and say, 'I am sorry. I should have knocked on the door.' But her eyes had travelled straight to a large box, wrapped in brown paper, on the round table.

'You should both be in bed. It is very very late.'

Edward was about to defend his cousin by pointing out that she should be excused because she was so excited about her birthday present, but Leonora had already gone to the table and put her hand on the box.

'Is this for me, is this it?'

There was a silence. Kestrel was tired, and wanted only to give the child her present and have them all go to bed but she saw Violet in the greedy little face, a carelessness about anyone or anything except herself, let alone even the most ordinary politeness. She knew that she ought to reprimand, to withhold the box until the next morning, to start however belatedly to control this strange, proud, self-centred child to whom she felt she had a vague responsibility.

But this was not the time and besides, she could not face whatever scene might follow.

'Yes, you may open it but after that you must go to bed or you will make yourself overwrought and ill.'

Leonora gave her a swift, ecstatic smile and then started to open the parcel but the string had difficult knots, so that Aunt Kestrel was obliged to find her small scissors. The child's eyes did not leave the parcel. Edward held his breath. He prayed for the doll to be like the one he had painted for her, as like as possible and if not, then every bit as grand.

The doll was in a plain oblong white box, tied with

red ribbon. Now Leonora held her breath too, her small fingers trembling as she unpicked the bow. Edward moved closer, wanting to see, wanting to close his eyes.

There was the rustle of layer after layer of tissue paper as she unwrapped each sheet very carefully. And then she came to the doll.

It was a baby doll, large and made of china, with staring blue eyes and a rosebud mouth in a smooth, expressionless face. It wore a white cotton nightdress and beside it was a glass feeding bottle.

Neither Edward nor Kestrel ever forgot the next moments. Leonora looked at the doll, her body rigid, her hands clenched. Then, with what sounded like a growl which rose in pitch from deep in her throat into her mouth and became a dreadful animal howl, she lifted it out of the box, turned and hurled it at the huge marble fireplace. It hit a carved pillar and there was a crack as it fell, one large piece and a few shards broken from the head to leave a jagged hollow, so that in his shock Edward wondered crazily if brains and blood might spill out and spread over the hearth tiles.

There was a silence so absolute and terrible that it seemed anything might have happened next, the house split down the middle or the ground open into a fiery pit, or one of them to drop down dead.

# I 2

LEONORA RAN. Her footsteps went thundering up the stairs and they could hear them, even louder, even faster, as she reached the top flights. The door of her bedroom slammed shut.

Aunt Kestrel seemed to have difficulty catching her breath and at last Edward said, 'I'm sure she didn't mean to be hurtful.'

She looked at him out of eyes whose centres were like brilliant pin-points of light but said nothing. Edward went to the doll in the hearth, picked it up, together with the broken pieces of china head, and trailed out, afraid to speak, even to glance at Aunt Kestrel.

The attic floor was dark and silent. He hesitated at Leonora's door and listened. She must have heard him come upstairs and stop and did not want to see him.

He went into his own room, carrying the doll, switched his bedside lamp on and sat down with it on his bed. The single large piece of china from its damaged head could probably be glued back, but the shards and fragments he thought were far too small. He sat holding it, wondering what he could do.

'Poor Dolly,' he said, holding it in his arms, rocking and stroking it.

The doll stared blankly, the crevasse in its china skull jagged, with cracks now running from it down the face like the spider cracks in walls. But he was bleary with tiredness and returned the doll to its box, put the lid back on and pushed it under his bed.

He slept restlessly, as if he had a fever, hearing the crack of the china doll hitting the fireplace and seeing Leonora's twisted, furious little face as she hurled it, and the wind howling through a crack in the window frame mingled with her scream. It was not yet midnight by his small travelling clock when he woke again. The wind still howled but in between he heard something else, fainter, and not so alarming.

He went out onto the landing. The wind was muffled and now he heard it more clearly he thought it was the sound of Leonora's crying. Her door was closed. Edward put his ear close to the wood. Silence. He waited. Still silence. He turned the handle slowly and eased open the door a very little. He could hear Leonora's very soft breathing but nothing else, no sobbing, no snuffling, nothing at all to show that she was crying now or had just been crying.

He could not go back to sleep, because of the wind and remembering the scene earlier, and because, when he lay down, he could hear the faint sound again. It was coming from beneath his bed, where the doll lay in its box. He sat bolt upright and shook his head to and fro hard to clear the sound but it had not gone away when he stopped. The wind was dying down and before long it died altogether and then his room was frighteningly silent except for the crying.

He was not a cowardly boy, though he had a natural cautiousness, but for a long time he lay, not daring to lean over and pull the box out from under the bed. He had no doubt that the sound came from it and he knew that he was awake, no longer in the middle of a nightmare, and that a china doll could not cry.

The crying went on.

When he gathered enough courage to open the box, taking the lid off slowly and moving each layer of tissue paper round the doll with great caution, he looked at the broken face and saw nothing, no fresh cracks or marks and above all, no tears and no changed expression to one of sadness or distress. The doll still stared out sightlessly and when he touched it the china was cold as cold.

He waited. Nothing. He covered the doll and moved it back out of sight. He lay down. The soft crying began again at once.

Edward got out of bed and switched on his lamp, took the box and without opening it again, carried it over to the deep cupboard and climbed onto a wooden stool. He put the box on the top shelf and pushed it as far to the back as he could, into the pitch darkness and dust.

'Now be quiet,' he said, 'please stop crying and be quiet.'

He lay still for a long time, his ears straining to hear the faintest sound from the cupboard. But there was none. The doll was silent.

# 13

FOR THE next three nights the doll cried until Aunt Kestrel asked Edward why he was white-faced with dark stains beneath his eyes, from lack of sleep. He said nothing to anyone and Leonora had spent little time with him. She had been in disgrace, forbidden to go outside, forbidden to have toys, kept to her room until she gave what Aunt Kestrel called 'a heartfelt apology'. Edward had crept in a couple of times and found her sitting staring out of the window, or lying on her back on the bed, not reading, not sleeping, just looking up at the ceiling. He had offered to stay, told her he was sorry, that he would ask Aunt Kestrel to let her come outside, suggested this or that he could bring to her. She had either not replied or shaken her head, but once, she had looked at him and said, 'Mrs Mullen said I was possessed by a demon. I think that may be true.'

He had told her demons did not exist, that she simply had a bad temper and would learn to overcome it, but she said it was not just a bad temper, it was an evil one. Mrs Mullen had brought her boiled fish, peas and a glass of water on a tray and told her she was bringing badness upon the house.

'I am, I am.'

'Don't be silly. I'm very bored. I wish you would apologise and then you could come out and we could do something, walk along the river and watch the lock open or look for herons.'

But she had yawned and turned away.

The doll cried for a fourth night and this time he climbed up to the shelf and took it down. It lay in its box, stiff and still, looking like a body in a coffin.

And realising that, he knew what he should do.

He was sure he should do it by himself. Leonora was likely to scream or have a fright, behave stupidly or tell Aunt Kestrel. The prospect only frightened him a little.

Leonora was allowed downstairs, though because she had stood in front of Aunt Kestrel with a mutinous face and refused to apologise, she was still forbidden the outside world.

\*     \*     \*

It was hot again, the sun blazing out of an enamel blue sky, the fens baked and the channels running dry but when Edward woke at five the air still had a morning damp and freshness. He dressed in shorts and shirt, and put on his plimsolls which made no noise.

He looked in the box. Dolly lay still in her tissue paper shroud, though he had heard the crying as he went to sleep and when he woke once in the night.

Someone would hear him, the stairs would creak, the door key would make a clink, the door would stick, as it did after rain. He waited, holding his breath, for Mrs Mullen to appear and ask what he was doing, or Aunt Kestrel to take the box and order him back to bed.

But he went stealthily, made no sound. No one heard him, no one came.

The road to the church was dusty under the early morning sun. Smoke curled from the chimney of the lock keeper's cottage beside the water. The dog barked. A heron rose from the river close beside him, a great pale ghost flapping away low over the fen.

He was afraid of the churchyard, afraid of the gnarled trunks of the yew trees and the soft swish of tall grasses against his legs. At the back, against the wall, the gravestones were half sunken into the earth, their stone lettering too worn away or moss-covered to read. No one left flowers here, no one cleared and tidied. No one remembered these ancient dead. He wondered about what was under the soil and inside the coffins, imagined skulls and bones stretched out.

He had brought a tin spade he had found in a cupboard. Its edge was rough and the wooden handle wobbled in its shaft and when he started trying to dig with it into the tussocks of grass he realised it would break before he had broken into the ground. But further along the grass petered out to thin soil and pine needles and using the spade and his hands, he dug out enough. It took a long time. His hands blistered quickly and the blisters split open and his arms tired. A thrush came and pecked at the soil he had uncovered and a wagon went down the road. He ducked behind the broad tree trunk.

When he came to bury the doll in its small cardboard coffin he thought he should say a prayer, as people always did at funerals, but it was not easy to think of suitable words.

'Oh God, let Dolly lie in peace without crying.'

He bowed his head. The thrush went on pecking at the soil, even after he had dragged it over the coffin and the grave with his tin spade.

When he slipped back into the house, he heard Mrs Mullen from the kitchen, and his aunt moving about her room. It was after seven o'clock.

\* \* \*

No one found out. No one took the slightest notice of him, he was of no account. A telegram had arrived saying that Leonora's mother was in London and waiting for her, she should be put on the train as soon as possible that day.

'I long for her,' Aunt Kestrel said, as she finished reading the telegram out.

Mrs Mullen, setting down the silver pot of coffee on its stand, made a derisive sound under her breath.

The morning was a scramble of boxes and trunks and people flying up and down the stairs. Edward went outside, afraid to be told that he was getting underfoot, the image of the silent, buried doll filling his mind. He did not know what he might do if Leonora asked for it.

She did not. She stood in the hall surrounded by her luggage, her hair tied back in a ribbon which made her look unfamiliar, already someone he did not know. He could not picture where she was going to, or imagine her mother and the latest stepfather.

'I will probably never see you again,' she said. The station taxi was at the door and Aunt Kestrel was putting on her hat, looking in her bag. She would see Leonora onto the train.

'You might,' Edward said. 'We are cousins.'

'No. Our mothers hated one another. I think we will be strangers.'

She put out a slender, cool hand and he shook it. He wanted to say something more, remind her of things they had said to one another, what had happened, what they had shared, to hold onto this strange, interesting holiday. But Leonora was already somewhere else and he sensed that she would not welcome such reminders.

He watched her walk, stiff-backed, down the path, her luggage stowed away in the taxi, Aunt Kestrel fussing behind her.

'Goodbye, Leonora,' he said quietly.

She did not look round, only climbed in to the taxi and sat staring straight ahead as the car moved off. She did not glance back at him, or at Iyot House, which he understood was for her already part of the past and moving farther and farther away as the taxi wheels turned.

The sound of the motor died away.

'And good riddance,' Mrs Mullen said from the hall. 'That's a bad one and brought nothing but bad with her, so be glad she's gone and pray she's left none of it behind her.'

Edward woke in the middle of the night to a deathly stillness, in the house and outside, and remembered that he was alone in the attics. Aunt Kestrel was two

90

floors below, Mrs Mullen in the basement. Leonora had gone.

He closed his eyes and tried to picture a sea of black velvet, which he had once been told was the way to bring on sleep, and after a time he did fall into drowsiness, but through it, in the distance, he heard the sound of paper rustling and the muffled crying of Dolly, buried beneath the earth.

# PART THREE

# 14

I WAS ABROAD when I had the letter telling of my Aunt Kestrel's death. She was over ninety and had been in a nursing home and failing for some time. I had always sent her birthday and Christmas cards and presents but I had seen her very little since the holidays I spent at Iyot as a boy and now, as one always does, I felt guilty that I had not made more effort to visit her in her old age. I am sure she must have been lonely. She was an intelligent woman with many interests and one who was happy in her own company. She was not a natural companion for a small boy but she had always done her best to ensure that I was happy when I stayed there and as I grew older I had been able to talk to her more about the things that interested her and which I was beginning to learn a little about – medieval history, military biography, the Fenlands, and her impeccable botanical illustrating.

I was saddened by her death and planned to return for her funeral but the day after I received the news, I had a letter from her solicitor informing me that Aunt Kestrel had given him strict and clear instructions that it was to be entirely private, followed by cremation, and so anxious had she been not to have any mourners that the day and time were being kept from everyone save those immediately involved and the lawyer himself. But he concluded:

'However, I have Mrs Dickinson's instructions that she wishes you and your cousin, Mrs Leonora Sebastian to attend my office, on a day to be arranged to your convenience, to be told the contents of her Will, of which I am the executor.'

I wrote to Leonora at the last address I had but I had had no contact with her for some years. I knew that she had married and been divorced and thought she sounded like her mother's daughter, but she had not replied to my last two cards and had apparently dropped out of sight.

Then, the evening I received the solicitor's letter, she telephoned me. I had just arrived back in London. She sounded as I might have expected, haughty and somewhat brusque.

'I suppose this is necessary, Edward? It's not convenient and I hate those bloody fens.'

'He wouldn't have asked us if he could have dealt with it any other way – he is almost certainly acting on Aunt Kestrel's instructions. I shall drive up. Would you like me to take you?'

'No, I'm not sure what arrangements I shall make. I want to see the house, do you? I presume we are the only legatees and we'll get everything? Though as I am older and my mother was older than yours, it would seem fairer that I get the lion's share.'

She left me speechless. We agreed to meet at Iyot House, and then again at the solicitor's the following morning. I wondered what she would look like now, whether she still had the wonderful flaring red hair, if she still had a temper, if she had married again and borne any children. I knew almost nothing about Leonora's adult life, as I imagined she knew little about mine. She would not have had enough interest in me to find out.

She had not, of course, turned up the previous evening at the house, and left no message. I daresay she couldn't be bothered. But that she would bother to attend the reading of our aunt's Will I had no doubt.

# 15

THE SOLICITOR'S office was everything one would have expected, housed in a small building in the Market Square of Cold Eeyle, which was probably Elizabethan and little changed, but the solicitor himself, a Mr James Maundeville, was quite unlike the person I had pictured. He had worked for his father and uncle, and then taken over the firm when both had retired. He was only in his late thirties, at a guess, and had a woman as junior partner.

'Mrs Sebastian is not here yet. Can I get you some coffee or would you prefer to wait until she arrives?'

I said that I would wait and we chatted about my aunt and Iyot House, while we looked out onto the Square, which was small, with shops and banks and businesses on two sides, the Town Hall and an open cobbled market on the other. It was a cold, windy morning with clouds scudding past the rooftops, but the fog had quite gone.

We chatted for perhaps ten minutes, and then Maundeville went out, saying he had something to sign. Another ten minutes went by. I was not surprised. It fitted in with everything I had known of Leonora that she should be so late and it was forty minutes after ten when I finally heard voices and footsteps on the stairs. Maundeville's secretary opened the door and said that he was on the telephone, apologised, and said that she would bring coffee in a couple of minutes.

I had wondered how much my cousin might have changed but as she walked into the room, I knew her at once. Her flaring red hair had softened in colour a little, but still sprang from her head in the old, commanding way; her face was as pale, though now made up and with a tautness at the sides of her eyes and jaw that indicated she had probably had a face lift. Her eyes were as scornful as ever, her hand as cool when she put it briefly into mine.

'Why are we being dragged to this godforsaken place when everything could easily have been sent in the post?'

She did not ask me how I was, tell me where she had come from, mention Aunt Kestrel.

I said I supposed the solicitor was following our

aunt's instructions and I heard again the short, hard little laugh I had got to know so well.

She sat down and glanced at me with little interest.

'God I hated that place,' she said. 'What on earth am I going to do with it? Sell it, that's the only possible thing, though whoever would be mad enough to want it? Do you remember those awful poky little rooms she gave us in the attics?'

'Yes. Do you . . .'

'And that woman . . . Mrs . . . pinch-face . . .'

'Mullen.'

'You were a very meek little boy.'

I did not remember myself as that, though I knew I had been intimidated by Leonora, and also quite careful in manner and behaviour, anxious not to cause any trouble.

'Quite the goody-goody.'

'Whereas you . . .'

The laugh again.

'God I hated it. Nothing to do, the wind howling, boring books, no games.'

'Oh but there were games – don't you remember playing endless Bagatelle?'

'No. I remember there was nothing to do at all.'

'You had your birthday while we were there.'

'Did I? What, eight, nine, something like that?'

'Nine.'

'Do you have children?'

'No, I'm afraid . . .'

'Nor do I yet but I'm expecting one, God help me.'

I must have looked startled.

'Yes, yes, I know, I'm forty-three, stupid thing to do.'

'Your husband . . .'

'Archer? American, of course. He's twenty years younger, so I suppose he ought to have a family but this will be it, he's lucky to get one.'

She told me that he was her third husband, an international hotelier, that they had flats in New York and Paris but spent most of the time travelling.

'I live in grand hotels, out of a suitcase. Where is the man?'

Every so often I caught sight of the child Leonora inside this brittle, well-dressed woman, but she was more or less completely masked by what, oddly, seemed to me a falsely adult air. I wondered if she still had terrors and a temper. I was about to find out.

James Maundeville came back, full of apologies. Leonora made a gesture of annoyance. He picked up a file on his desk, and took out the usual long envelope in which solicitors file Last Will and Testaments.

'I won't read the preamble; it's just the familiar disclaimers. Mrs Dickinson had savings and investments which formed the capital on whose interest she lived for many years but that capital was considerably eroded by the needs of her last year in a nursing home. The remainder amounts to some twelve thousand pounds. There are no valuables – a few items of personal jewellery worth perhaps a thousand pounds all told. But she expressly asked that you should both, as her sole legatees, come here to learn not so much what she has left but the somewhat – er – eccentric – conditions attached. I did not draw up Mrs Dickinson's will, my father did and I'm afraid he has been suffering from dementia for the last eighteen months and so I wasn't able to discuss this with him.'

He looked up at us both. His face was serious but there was a flicker of amusement there too. He was a good looking, pleasant man with a strong trace of the local accent in his educated voice.

Leonora sat with one stockinged leg crossed tightly over the other. I tried to imagine her as the mother of a child, but simply could not. I felt sorry for any offspring she might produce.

'Mrs Dickinson left her entire estate, which includes everything I mentioned above – the money, pieces of jewellery and so on, plus Iyot House, with all its contents – with an exception which I will come to –' He cleared his throat nervously, and hesitated a

moment before continuing, 'to Mr Edward Cayley . . .'
A glance at me.

'The exception . . .'

But before he could read on, Leonora let out an animal cry of rage and distress. I had heard it once before.
The voice was older, the tone a little deeper, but other-
wise her furious howl was exactly the same as the one
she had uttered the night of her birthday when she
had opened the doll Aunt Kestrel had brought for her
from London.

Mr Maundeville looked alarmed. I got up, and took
Leonora's arm but she shook me off and raged at us
both, her words difficult to make out but not difficult
to guess at. He proffered water, but then simply sat
waiting for the outburst to run its course.

Leonora was like someone possessed. She raged
against Aunt Kestrel, me, the solicitor, raged about
unfairness and deceit and hinted at fraud and collu-
sion. The house should have been hers, the estate hers,
though we could not discover why she was so sure.
Desire, want, getting what she believed ought to be
hers – simple greed, these were what drove her, as they
had driven her in childhood and, I saw now, through-
out her life.

In the end, I persuaded her to calm and quieten by

saying that whatever Aunt Kestrel had willed, once the estate was mine I could do what I liked and there was no question of not sharing things with her fairly. This stopped her.

Mr Maundeville had clearly formed a poor impression of Leonora and wanted her out of his sight. He went back to the Will.

'Mrs Dickinson has left one item to you, Mrs Sebastian. I confess I do not fully understand the wording.

'My niece Leonora should have the china doll which was my 9th birthday gift to her and for which she was so ungrateful, in the hope that she will learn to treat it, as she should treat everyone, with more kindness and care.'

He sat back and laid down the paper. Leonora's hands were shaking, her face horribly pale and contorted with fury. But she said no word. She got up and walked out, leaving me to smooth things over, explain and apologise as best I could and follow her into the square.

She was nowhere to be seen. I wandered about for some time looking for her but in the end I gave up, and drove back out to Iyot House. Of course, I intended to share my inheritance with Leonora. I could not in conscience have done anything else, though she had made me angry and tempted me to change my mind and keep everything, simply out of frustration at her behavior. She was the child she had been and if no one else could bring her face to face with her unpleasant character, perhaps I could.

But whatever I decided, I was determined that she should have the wretched doll. As I drove across the fen something was hovering just under the surface of my mind, as it had been hovering all the previous night, but when I had heard Maundeville read out the clause about the doll, something had bubbled nearer to the surface, and I had remembered Leonora's outburst that terrible evening, Aunt Kestrel's hurt and annoyance, and then something else, something closer to me, or rather, to my eight-year-old self.

The sun was shining and there was a brisk breeze. As I went towards the gates to the yard, I saw that they had been opened already and that a large car was parked there. Leonora was ahead of me.

The house felt cold and bleak, and smelled more strongly of dust and emptiness than I had remembered from the previous day. I went inside and called out. At first, there was no reply, but as I went up the stairs, calling again, I heard Leonora's voice.

She was in the attics, standing at the window of her old room, looking down.

'How weird,' she said. 'It's smaller and dingier than I remember and it reeks of unhappiness.'

'Not mine,' I said, 'I was never unhappy here though I

was sometimes bored and sometimes lonely. But I thought you and I had quite a happy time that summer.'

She shook her head, not so much in disagreement as if she were puzzled.

'Did you understand that nonsense about a doll?' She spoke dismissively.

'Anyhow, why should I care tuppence about it, whatever she meant? The old woman was obviously demented. But now, I suggest the only thing to be done here is for you to sell the house and divide the money between us. God knows, I wouldn't want to come back again and I doubt if you do.'

But I had stopped listening to her. We were in my old attic room now and I had seen the cupboard in the wall again. And I remembered I had first hidden the doll there. I stood transfixed, a small boy lying in the bed and hearing the rustle of the tissue paper. I was looking again inside the white cardboard box and seeing the smashed china head and the blue, sightless yet staring eyes, and feeling sorry for the doll even though, like my cousin, I did not care for it very much. I had been frightened too, for what doll could cry, let alone move so that its tissue covering rustled?

She had gone back down the stairs and I could hear her snapping up one of the blinds in Aunt Kestrel's sitting room.

'Come on,' I said, 'I know where it is.'

'What are you babbling about now?'

But I was out and down the path to the gate. I called back to her over my shoulder. 'I'm going to get it for you.'

I was not in control of myself. I felt pushed on by the urge to find out if I was right, get the doll and give it back to Leonora, as if I could never rest again until I did. It seemed to be the doll that was urging me, demanding to be rescued and returned to its owner, but I knew now that it, or perhaps, the memory of it, had possessed me for all those years. I felt partly that I wanted to be rid of all trace of it, partly responsible because only I knew where it was and could rescue it. I did not pause to consider how sane this all was, or that I was behaving bizarrely, a man in his forties who had never before been under the influence of something I could only fear was other than human.

# 16

'Edward? where are you? What in God's name are you doing?'

'Here. Over here.'

Dusk was rapidly gathering now, the sky still light on the horizon, but the land darkening. I had reached the churchyard and was clambering over the hassocks of thick grass and the prone gravestones, to reach the low stone wall. I could hear Leonora calling after me and then her footsteps coming down the path but I did not wait. I knew what I must do and she was no longer any part of it. I was acting alone and under the urging of something quite other.

I found what I thought was the nearest gravestone and then, to my surprise, the patch of soil that no grass had managed to invade. There were pine needles and a few small fir cones. It was hard and bone dry there and I had nothing with which to dig but my own bare hands. But I knelt down and started to scrabble away at the surface.

Leonora appeared beside me, breathing hard, as if she had been running, but more out of fear than exertion I knew.

'Edward?'

'I have to do this. I have to do it.'

'Do what? Dig a hole? Find something down there?'

'Both.' I sat back on my heels. 'But it's hopeless; I can make no impression at all. I need a spade.' And I remembered the feel of the small tin spade in my hands, the blunted, rusty edge with which I had dug into this same ground. I cannot have gone down far.

I got up and went round the side of the church, finding what I needed almost at once – the shed in which whoever maintained the churchyard and dug the occasional grave kept his things. The padlock was undone. I found what I needed easily enough, wondering how much it was used; Iyot Lock was a hamlet of so few houses – there cannot have been many burials.

Leonora had followed me, obviously not wanting to be alone, and now was beside the wall, looking down. I pushed the blade into the earth with all my strength but it was extremely hard ground and yielded little. I scraped away as best I could, and after a short time the soil loosened. There were some tree roots which must have spread in the many years since I was last here and which made my task harder but I did not have to go very deep before I bumped against something caught beneath one of them. It was not hard, but felt compressed. I threw down the space and knelt on the grass. Leonora was standing nearby, and as I glanced up I saw that she was looking with alarm at me, as if she feared I had gone mad.

'It's all right,' I said, in a falsely cheerful voice, 'I told you I would find it for you.'

'Find what? What on earth are you doing, Edward, and should you be digging about in a churchyard? Isn't that wickedness or illegal or some such thing? You could be digging up someone's grave.'

'I am,' I said.

It seems insane indeed, now I look back, but at the time I was possessed by the need to find out if I was right, and get Leonora what my aunt had willed her. She was right, as she had screeched in the solicitor's office, she had been cut out of the rest of the inheritance and only left the wretched doll in what was perhaps the one mean-spirited gesture our aunt had ever made. Her childhood behaviour over the birthday doll, her spoilt tantrum and violent rejection of it, when Kestrel had gone to buy it especially, to make up for disappointment, must have rankled for years – unless she had written her will shortly after it had all happened. Either way, she intended Leonora to be taught a lesson but I was not going to indulge in that sort of tit-for-tat gesture. I would tell Leonora that I planned to give her exactly half the money we eventually achieved.

This had all become some sort of game that had gone too far. I knew that well enough as I knelt on the ground and felt around with both my hands in the space under the tree root. I soon came upon a damp lump of something and gradually used my fingers to ease it away from the soil.

The white cardboard box had rotted away over the years and then adhered like clay to the contents, and as I took it in my hands, I could feel the shape beneath. It was a slimy grey mess.

It was also almost completely dark and I laid the object on the ground while I hastily covered the soil back over the shallow place I had cleared.

'Come on, back to the house. I can't see anything here.'

'Edward, what have you done?'

'I told you – I have retrieved your inheritance.'

I carried it carefully down the dark road back to Iyot House. It felt unpleasant, slimy and with clots of soil adhering to the wet mush of cardboard.

I do not know that I had thought particularly about the state the doll would be in after being buried for so long. Certainly the way the box had disintegrated was no surprise – the very fact that it was there at all was remarkable. If you had asked me I suppose I would have said the doll would be very dirty, perhaps unrecognisable as a doll, but undamaged – china or pot or plastic, whatever it was actually made of, would not have rotted like the box.

I went into the old kitchen, found a dust sheet and laid it on the deal table. Leonora seemed to be as intrigued as I was, though also distinctly alarmed.

'How did you know where to look? What on earth was it doing buried there in the churchyard?'

I half remembered that something had happened to startle me and make me want the wretched thing out of the house but the details were hazy now.

'I think I had a dream about it.'

'Don't be ridiculous.'

But now we were both looking at the filthy soil-coated object on the table. I found a bowl of cold water, an ancient cloth and a blunt kitchen knife and began to rinse and scrape away carefully.

'I don't know why you are doing this. Is it full of money?'

'I doubt it.'

'No, of course it isn't. I don't want it, can't you understand Edward? This is a stupid game. For God's sake, throw it in a bin and let's get out of this awful house.'

All the same, she could not help watching me intently as I worked patiently away. It did not take me long to get rid of the wet sodden mush of soil and cardboard and then my fingers touched the hard object beneath. I emptied and re-filled the bowl of water and rinsed and re-rinsed. First the body of the china doll appeared, dirty but apparently intact.

'I know Aunt Kestrel would have wanted you to have it in as near perfect condition as we can get it, Leonora!'

She was transfixed by the sight. 'I remember it,' she said after a moment. 'It's coming back to me – that awful night. I remember expecting it to be something so special, so beautiful, and this hideous china baby came out of the box.'

'Do you remember what kind of a doll you had wanted? I drew a picture of it for you.'

She told me, though some of the detail was inaccurate, but the bridal princess came to life as she spoke.

I was anxious not to damage this doll, so I worked even more slowly as I got most of the outer dirt away and then I carried it to the tap and rinsed it under a trickle of water. If I had stopped to think how ridiculous I must have looked – how oddly we were both

113

behaving indeed, perhaps I would not have gone on. I wish now that indeed I had not, that I had left the doll covered and buried under the earth in its sorry grave. But it was too late for that.

'There,' I said at last. 'Let us see your treasure, Leonora!' I spoke in a light and jocular tone, the last time I was to do so that night and for many others.

I carried the doll, still wet but clean, to the table and laid it down directly under the light. I had pushed all the rubbish into a bin so there was now just the scrubbed, pale wooden table top and the doll lying on it.

We both looked. And then Leonora's hand flew to her mouth as she made a dreadful low sound, not a cry, not a wail, hardly a human sound but something almost animal.

I looked into the face of the doll and then I too saw what she had seen.

When we had both looked at it last we were children and the doll was a baby doll, with staring bright blue eyes, a painted rosebud mouth and a smooth china face, neck, arms, legs and body. It was an artificial-looking thing but it was as like a human baby as any doll can ever be.

Now, we both stared in horror at the thing on the table in front of us. It was not a baby, but a wizened old woman, a crone, with a few wisps of twisted greasy grey hair, a mouth slightly open to reveal a single black tooth, and the face gnarled and wrinkled like a tree trunk, with lines and pockmarks. It was sallow, the eyes were sunken and the lids creased with age, the lips thin and hard.

I let out a small cry, and then said, 'But of course. This isn't your doll. Someone has changed it for this hideous thing.'

'How,' Leonora asked in a whisper, 'When? Why? Whoever knew it had been buried there?'

I would have tried to come up with a thousand explanations but I could not even begin. For as I looked at the dreadful, aged doll, I realised that the crack in the skull and the hollow beneath it, which had come when Leonora had hurled it at the wall, were exactly the same, still jagged like a broken egg, though dirty round the edges from being in the earth.

This was not a replacement doll, put there by someone – though God knows who – with a sick sense of humour. This was the first doll, the bland-faced baby. The crack in its skull was exactly as it had been, I was sure of that. The body was the same size and shape though oddly crooked and with chicken-claw hands and feet and a yellow, loose-skinned neck. This was the doll Aunt Kestrel had given Leonora. It was the same doll.

But the doll had grown old.

\* \* \*

I managed to find some brandy in Aunt Kestrel's old sitting-room cupboard, and poured us both a generous glassful. After that, I locked up the house, leaving everything as it was, and drove Leonora back to Cold Eeyle and the hotel, for she was in no state to do anything for herself. She sat beside me shaking and occasionally letting out a little cry, after which her body would give a long convulsive shudder. I insisted that a doctor be called out, as she was in the early stages of pregnancy, and stayed until he had left, saying that she needed sleep and peace but that she and the child were essentially unharmed.

I spent a terrible night, full of nightmares in which dolls, old ones and young ones mixed together, came at me out of thick fog, alternately laughing and crying. I woke at six and went straight out, driving fast to Iyot House through a drear, cold morning.

The doll which had grown old was where we had left it, on the kitchen table, and still old and wizened, like a witch from a fairy tale. I had half expected to find that it had all been some dreadful illusion and that the doll was still a baby, just filthy and distorted by having been buried in the damp earth for so long.

But the earth had done nothing to the doll, other than ruining its cardboard coffin. The doll was a crone, looking a hundred years old or a thousand, ancient and repulsive.

I did as I had done before, went alone to the church-yard and buried it, this time wrapped in an old piece of sheeting. I dug as deep as I could and replaced the earth firmly on top. When I had finished I felt a sense of release. Whatever had happened, the wretched, hideous thing would never emerge again and there was an end.

But she had power to haunt me. I dreamed of the aged doll for many nights, many months. I worried over what had happened and how. Sometimes, I half convinced myself that we had both imagined it, Leonora and I, for, of course, an inanimate object, a doll made of pot, could not age. The dirt and soil, added to years in the damp ground, had changed the features – that was quite understandable.

In the end, the image faded from my mind and reason took over.

Leonora disappeared from my life once more, though I heard in a roundabout way that she had returned to the Far East and her hotelier husband.

As for me, I was about to pack up Iyot House and put it up for sale, when I was asked to go abroad myself, to do a special job for a foreign government and it was such a major and exciting challenge that the house in the fens and everything to do with it went from my mind.

# PART FOUR

# 17

I WAS TO spend three or four months in the city of Szargesti, a once-handsome place in the old Eastern Europe. It had an old and beautiful centre, but much of that had been demolished during the 1970s, to make way for wide roads on which only presidential and official cars could travel, vast, ugly new civic buildings and a monstrous presidential palace. The Old Town was medieval, and had once housed a jewellery quarter, book-binders and small printers, leather workers, and various tradesmen who kept the ancient buildings upright. Many had been wood and lathe, with astonishing painted panels on their façades. There had been a cathedral and other old churches, as well as a synagogue, for a large section of the original population of Szargesti had been Jewish. The place had been vandalised and the demolition had proceeded in a brutal and haphazard fashion, along-side the hurried erection of a new civic centre. But the Prague Spring had come to Szargesti, the president had been exiled, many of his cronies executed, and both demolition and building had come to an abrupt halt. Huge craters stood in the middle of streets, blocks of flats were left half in ruins, the machinery which had been pulling them down left rusting in their midst. It was a testament to grand designs and the lust for power of ignorant men. I am an adviser on the conservation of ancient buildings and sometimes, on whole areas, as in the case of Szargesti. My task was to identify and catalogue what was left, photograph it and make certain that nothing else was destroyed, and then to give the city advice on how to shore up, pre-serve, rebuild with care.

I knew that the Old Town, with its medieval buildings – houses, shops, workshops – was the most important area and in urgent need of conservation and repair. I had quickly come to love the place, with its small, intimate squares, narrow cobbled alleyways, beautiful, often ramshackle four-storey buildings with their neglected but still beautiful frescoes and wall paint-ings. The best way of getting to know a place is simply to wander and this is almost all I did for the first couple of weeks, taking dozens of photographs. Every evening I returned to my hotel to make copious notes, but after I had come to know the city a little better I would often stay out late, find a café in the back streets, drink a beer or a coffee and watch what little street life there was. People were still uncertain, ground down by years of a brutal dictatorship and most of them kept safely inside their homes after dark. But one warm summer evening I went into the Old Town and a square I had chanced upon earlier in the day, and which had some of the most beautiful and undamaged houses I had so far discovered. It would once have housed traders and craftsmen in precious metals whose workshops were situated beneath their houses. On the corner I passed an old stone water trough with an elaborately carved iron tap stood beside it. Horses would have drunk here, but the water had probably also been carried away in buckets, for use in smelting.

Now, the heavy wooden doors and iron shutters of the workshops were closed and some were padlocked, and those padlocks were rusty and broken. Many of the upper rooms had gaping dark spaces where windows had fallen out.

There was a small café with a few tables on the cobbles. The barman appeared the moment I sat down, brought my drink and a small dish of smoked sausage, but then returned to the doorway and watched me until I began to feel uneasy. I had no need to be, I knew, and I tried to enjoy the quietness, the last of the sunshine and the way the shadows lengthened, slipping across the cobbles towards me. The old women who had been sitting on a bench chatting, left. The tobacconist came out with a long pole and rattled down his shutters. The beer was good. The sausage tasted of woodsmoke.

I continued to feel uneasy and strangely restless, alone in the darkening square. So far as I knew, only the waiter was looking at me but I had the odd sense that there were others, watching from the blanked-out windows and hidden corners. I have always believed that places with a long history, especially those in which terrible events have taken place, retain something of those times, some trace in the air, just as I have been in many a cathedral all over the world and sensed the impress of centuries of prayers and devotions. Places are often filled with their own pasts and exude a sense of them, an atmosphere of great good or great evil, which can be picked up by anyone sensitive to their surroundings. Even a dog's hackles can rise in places reputed to be haunted. I am not an especially credulous man but I believe in these things because I have experienced them. I am not afraid of the dark and it was not the evening shadows that were making me nervous now. Certainly I had no fear of potential attackers or of spies leftover from the city's past. Thank God those days were over and Szargesti was struggling to come to terms with the new freedoms.

I finished my beer and got up.

The air was still warm and the stars were beginning to brighten in the silky sky as I walked slowly round the square, where the cobbles gave way to stone paving. Every window was dark and shuttered. The only sound was that of my own footsteps.

Here and there an old stable door stood ajar, revealing cobbles on which straw was still scattered though the horses had long gone. I passed a music shop, a cobbler's, and one tiny frontage displaying pens and parchment. All were locked up, and dark. Then, in the middle of the narrowest, dimmest alley, where the walls of the houses bulged across almost to meet one another, I saw a yellowish light coming from one of the windows and nearing it, I found a curious shop.

The window was dusty, making it difficult to see much of what was inside but I could make out shelves and an ancient counter. No attempt had been made to display goods attractively – the window held a jumble of objects piled together. I put my hand on the latch and at once heard the ring of an old-fashioned bell.

A very small old man was behind the mahogany counter, his skin paper pale and almost transparent over the bones of his cheeks and skull. He had tufts of yellow-white hair, yellow-white eyebrows and a jeweller's glass screwed into one eye, with which he was examining a round silver box, dulled and stained with verdigris.

He raised a finger in recognition of my entrance, but continued to peer down at the object, and so I looked round me at the stock, which was crammed onto the shelves, spilled out of drawers, displayed in glass cabinets. The floor was of uncovered oak boards, polished and worn by the passage of feet over years.

The lower shelves contained small leather bound books, boxes of various sizes with metal hasps, dulled by the same verdigris as the box being scrutinised, wooden trays with what looked like puzzles fitted into them, a couple of musical boxes. Higher up, I saw wooden cabinets with sets of narrow drawers, each labelled in the old Cyrillic alphabet which had not been used in the country for almost a century. A doll's house stood on the floor beside me, its eaves and roof modelled on those of the buildings in the square, its front hanging half-off its single hinge. Beside it was a child-sized leather trunk, the leather rubbed and lifting here and there. I glanced at the old man but now he had set the box on a scrap of dark blue velvet set down on the counter and was peering at it even more intently through his eyeglass, I thought perhaps trying to make out some pattern or inscription.

I turned back to the doll's house and trunk and as I did so, I heard a sound which at first I took to be the scratching of a mouse in the skirting somewhere – I hoped a mouse, and not a rat. It stopped and then, as I put out my hand to touch the front of the wooden house, started again, and though it was still very soft, I knew that it was not the noise made by any sort of rodent. I could not tell exactly where it originated – it seemed to be coming from the darkness somewhere, behind me, or to one side – I could not quite pin down the direction. It was a rustling of some kind – perhaps the sound made when the wind blows through branches or reeds, perhaps the movement of long grass. Yet it was not altogether like those sounds. It stopped again. I looked at the old man but he was crouching over his box, his narrow back half bent, shoulders hunched.

I waited. It came again. A soft, insistent, rustling sound. Like paper. Someone was rustling paper – perhaps sheets of tissue paper. I turned my head to one corner, then the other but the sound did not quite come from there, or there, or from anywhere.

Perhaps it was inside my own head.

The old man sat up abruptly, put down the eyeglass and looked directly at me. His eyes were the watery grey of the sea on a dull day, dilute and pale.

'Good evening,' he said in English. 'Is it something special you look for, because in a moment, I close.'

'Thank you, no. I was just interested to find a shop here and open at this time.'

'Ah.'

'You sell many different things. What do you call yourself?'

'A restorer.'

'But so am I!'

'Toys?'

'No, ancient buildings. Like those in this quarter. I'm an architectural conservator.'

He nodded.

'Little is beyond repair but my job is more easy than yours.'

He gestured round. I had begun to notice that many of the objects on his shelves and even standing around the floor were old toys, mostly of wood, some painted elaborately, some simply carved. As well as the dolls' house I had already seen, there were others, and then a fort, many soldiers in the original military uniforms of the country's past, a wooden truck, a railway engine and many boxes of different sizes and shapes. A lot of them had clearly been gathering dust for years. I looked down at the cloth on which the miniature silver box was standing.

'This has been chased by hand, the most expert hand.' He offered the eyeglass for me to examine it. 'The work of a fine craftsman. It was found on the dresser of a dolls' house – but I think it was not a toy item. Please, look.'

I did so. There was some intricate patterning forming the border and in the centre, a night sky with moon and stars and clouds, with a swirl of movement suggesting a wild wind.

'Certainly not a toy.' I handed back the eyeglass. 'Marvellous workmanship.'

'This old part of Szargesti were craftsmen who worked in silver many years past, special craftsmen who passed down their skill to younger ones. Now . . .' he sighed. 'Almost none left. Skills in danger of death. I do not have these skills. I am only repairer of toys. Please, look round. You have some children?'

I shook my head. I assumed that everything here was waiting for repair and not for sale but even old toys, like many other domestic artefacts, tell a conservator something about the times in which they were made and even of the buildings in which they belonged and I poked about a little more, finding treasures behind treasures. But I wondered how long some of them had been lying here and how much longer they would have to wait for the mender's attention. And then I wondered if some of the children who had owned and played with them were now grown-up or even dead, the toys were so old-fashioned.

The old man let me look around, poke into corners,

touch and even pick things up without taking any notice of me and I was at the very back of the shop, where it was even darker and dustier, when I heard it again. The faint rustling sound seemed to be coming from something close to me but when I turned, became softer as if it were moving away. I stood very still. The shop was quiet. I heard the rustling again, as if tissue paper were being scrumpled up or unfolded, and now I thought I could trace the sound to somewhere on the floor and quite close to my feet. I bent down but it was very dark and I saw nothing unusual, and there was no quick movement of a rodent scuttling away. It stopped. Started again, more softly. Stopped. I took a step or two forwards and my foot bumped up against something. I bent down. A cardboard box, about the size to contain a pair of boots, was just in front of me, the lid apparently tied on with stout string. It was as I put my hand out to touch it that I felt an iciness down my spine, and a sudden moment of fear. I was sure that I was remembering something but I had no idea what. Deep in my subconscious mind a cardboard box like this one had a place but in what way or from what stage of my life I did not know.

I stood up hastily and as I did so, the rustling began again. It was coming from inside the box.

But I did not have a chance to try to trace the source

of the sound, even if I was sure that I wanted to do so, because the old man unnerved me by saying:

'You are looking for a doll I think.'

I opened my mouth to say that I was not, had just been drawn into the shop out of curiosity, but I realised that was not true.

'Look there.'

I looked. In a cabinet just above my head was the doll, the exact, the same doll, which Leonora had yearned for all those years ago, the doll she had described in such detail and which I had tried to draw for her as some sort of compensation.

The Indian Princess, in her rich garments, shining jewels, sequins, beads, embroidery, sparkling with gold and silver, ruby and emerald, pearl and diamond, was sitting on some sort of velvet chair with a high, crested back, her face bland and serene, her veil sprinkled with silver and gold suns, moons and stars. She was not a doll for a child, not a doll to be played with, dressed and undressed, fed and pushed about in an old pram, she was far too fine, too regal, too formal. But I knew that this was the doll my cousin had yearned for so desperately and that I had no choice but to buy it – it had been placed here for just that reason. Even as the thought flashed across my mind, I was almost embarrassed, it was so ridiculous, and yet some part of me believed that it was true.

131

The old man was still tapping away calmly, smiling a little.

'Are your dolls for sale?'

'You wish to buy that one.' It was not a question.

He glanced at me, the very centres of his eyes steel-bright, fixed and all-seeing.

Now, he had come round the counter and was unlocking the cabinet. A shiver rippled down my back as he reached inside and took hold of the Indian Princess. He did not ask me if this was the one I wanted, simply took it down, locked the cabinet again and then laid the doll on the counter.

'I have the exact box.' He retreated into the shadows where I could just make out a door that stood ajar. My back was icy cold now. The shop was very quiet and somewhere in that quietness, I heard the rustling sound again.

He came back with the doll, boxed, lidded, tied with string and handed it over to me. I paid him and fled, out into the alley under the tallow light of the gas lamp, the coffin-like box under my arm. Through the window, I could make out the old man, behind the counter. He did not look up.

When I got back to the hotel, I pushed the doll under the bed in my room and went down to the cheerful bar, with its red shaded lamps and buzz of talk, and had a couple of brandies to try to rid myself of the unpleasant chill through my body, and a general sense of malaise. Gradually, I calmed. I began to try to work out why I had heard the rustling sound and what it had meant, but soon gave up. It could not have had anything to do with any of the similar sounds I had heard before. I was in another country, a different place.

I went to bed, fortified by the brandy, and was on the very cusp of sleep when I sat straight up, my heart thumping in my chest. The rustling sound had started up again and as I listened in horror, I realised that it was coming from close to hand. I lay down again and then it was louder. I sat up, and it faded.

Either the rustling was in my own head – or rather, in my ears, some sort of tinnitus – or it was coming from underneath the bed.

That night my dreams were full of cascading images of dolls, broken, damaged, buried, covered in dirt, labelled, lying on shelves, being hammered and glued and tapped. In the middle of it all, the memory of Leonora's twisted and angry face as she hurled the unwanted doll at the fireplace, and floating somewhere behind, the old man with the gimlet eyes.

I woke in a sweat around dawn and pulled the box from under the bed where I had left it, the string still carefully knotted. I did not want it in my sight, but I was sure that if I disposed of the doll I would have cause to regret it and first thing the next morning I took it to the post office. I had addressed it to myself in London but changed my mind at the last moment, and sent it instead to Iyot House. The reasons were mainly practical yet I was also sending the doll there because it seemed right and where it naturally belonged.

I felt relief when it was out of my hands. I had kept it and yet I had not.

# 18

Some months passed, during which I heard via an announcement in *The Times* that Leonora had given birth to a daughter. I returned to England, but for the next year or so I was constantly travelling between London and Szargesti, absorbed in my work and I gave thought to little else.

And then I received a letter from the solicitor, telling me that Leonora wished to be in touch with me urgently. She had written via Iyot House but received no reply. Might he forward my address to her?

By the time I did receive a letter, I was married, I had finished my work in Szargesti, and embarked on a new project connected with English cathedrals. Leonora was far from my mind.

Dear Edward

I write to you from the depths of despair. I am unsure how much you know of what has happened to me since we last met. Briefly, I have a daughter, who is now two years old, and named Frederica, after her father and my beloved husband, Frederic, who died very suddenly. We were in Switzerland. In short, he has left me penniless; the hotels are on the verge of bankruptcy thanks to bad advice. I did not know a thing. How could I have known when Frederic protected me from everything? And now my daughter has a grave illness.

I have nowhere to go, nowhere to live. I am staying with friends out of their kindness and pity but that must come to an end.

In short, I am throwing myself on your generosity and asking if you would allow me to have Iyot House in which to live, though God knows I hate the place and would not want to set foot inside it again, if this were not my only possible home. Perhaps we could make it habitable.

If you have already disposed of it then I ask if you could share some of the proceeds with me so that I can buy a place in which my sick child and I can live.

Please reply c/o the poste restante address and tell me urgently what you can do. We are cousins, after all,

Affectionately
Leonora.

I had done nothing about Iyot House and after I told my wife the gist of the story she agreed at once that, of course, Leonora and her daughter should live there for as long as they wished.

'It's been locked up for years. I don't know what state it will be in and it was never the most – welcoming of houses anyway.'

'But surely you can get people to go in and make sure it is clean and that there hasn't been any damage ... that the place isn't flooded? Then she can make the best of it ... Anything other than being homeless.'

I agreed but wondered as I did so if Leonora had told me the full truth, if she had indeed been left literally penniless and without the means to put a roof over her head. Her letter was melodramatic and slightly hysterical, entirely in character. Catherine chided me with heartlessness when I tried to explain and perhaps she was right. But then, she did not know Leonora.

Nevertheless, I wrote and said that she could have the house, that I would put anything to rights before she arrived, and would come to see her when I could manage it.

I had to travel to Cambridge a few days later, and I arranged to make a detour via Iyot House. It was September, the weather golden, the corn ripe in the fields, the vast skies blue with mare's tail clouds streaked high. At this time of year the area is so open, so fresh-faced, with nothing hidden for miles, everything was spread out before me as I drove. It is still an isolated place. No one has developed new housing clusters and the villages and hamlets remain quite self-contained, not spreading, not even seeming to relate to one another. Apart from some drainage, square miles had not changed since I was an eight-year-old boy being driven from the railway station on my first visit to Iyot House. I remembered how I had felt – interested and alert to my surroundings, and yet also lonely and apprehensive, determined but fearful. And when I had first glimpsed the place, I had shivered, though I had not known why. It was as though nothing was exactly as it seemed to be, like a place in a story, there were other dimensions, shadows, secrets, the walls seemed to be very slightly crooked. I was not an especially imaginative child, so I was even more aware of what I felt.

The house smelled of dust and emptiness but not, to my surprise, of damp or mould, and although everything seemed a little more faded and neglected, there was no interior damage. I pulled up some of the blinds and opened a couple of windows. A bird had fallen down one of the chimneys and its body lay in the empty fireplace, grass sprouted on window ledges. But the place was just habitable, if I found someone to clean and reorder it. Leonora would at least have a roof over her head for however long she and the child needed it.

I had noticed that the box I had sent from Szargesti was in the porch, tucked safely out of the weather. I took it inside and decided that I would place it upstairs in the small room off the main bedroom which Leonora might well choose for her daughter. The attics were too far away and lonely for a small child.

I put the box on the shelf, hesitating about whether to take the doll out and display it, or leave it as a surprise. In the end I removed all the outer wrapping and string, but left the box closed, so that the little girl could have the fun of opening it.

# 19

I HAVE WRITTEN this account in a reasonably calm, even detached frame of mind. I have remembered that first strange childhood visit to Iyot House in some detail without anxiety and although it distressed me a little to recall the unpleasantness over the doll with the aged face, its burial and exhumation, and Leonora's violent tempers, I have written with a steady hand. Events were peculiar, strange things happened, and yet I have looked back steadily and without falling prey to superstitions and night terrors. I have always believed that the odd happenings could be put down to coincidence or perhaps the effects of mood and atmosphere. I suppose I believed myself to be a rational man.

But reason does not help me now that I come to the climax of the story, and as I remember and as I write, I feel as if there is no ground beneath my feet, that I might disintegrate at any moment, that my flesh will dissolve. I feel afraid but I do not know of what. I feel helpless and at the mercy of strange events and forces which not only can I not explain away but in which I do not believe.

Yet what happened, happened, all of it, and the end lies in the beginning, in our childhood. But the blame is not mine, the blame is all Leonora's.

Work preoccupied me and then Catherine and I took a trip to New York, so that I was not in touch with Leonora until she had been living in Iyot House for some weeks.

It was one day in December when I had finished some more work in Cambridge earlier than I had expected, and I decided to drive across to Iyot House and either beg a bed for the night there or carry on to the inn at Cold Eeyle. I tried to telephone my cousin in advance but there was no reply and so I simply set off. It was early dusk and the sun was flame and ruby red in the clearest of skies as I went towards the fens. Once off the trunk roads, it was as quiet as ever. There were few lock keeper's cottages occupied now – that had been the one major change since my boyhood – but here and there a light glowed through windows, and the glint of these or of the low sun touched the black deep slow-running waters in river and dyke. The church at Iyot Lock stood out as a beacon in the flat landscape for miles ahead, the last of the sun touching its gilded flying angels on all four corners of the tower.

It was beautiful and seemed so serene an aspect that I was moved and felt happier to be coming here than ever before. So much of what we imagine is a product of an ill mood, a restless night, indigestion, or the vagaries of the weather and I began to feel certain that all the previous events at Iyot House had been caused by one or other of these, or by other equally fleeting outside circumstances. Empty houses breed fantasies, bleak landscapes lend themselves to fearful imaginings. Only lie awake on a windy night and hear a branch tap-tap-tapping on a casement to understand at once what I mean.

I drew up outside the house – the gate to the back entrance was locked and barred, so I parked in the road and got out. There was a light on in the sitting room, behind drawn curtains, one upstairs and possibly one at the very back. I did not want to startle Leonora, for she would presumably not expect callers on an early December evening, so I banged the door of the car shut a couple of times, and made some noise opening the gate and tramping up the path to the front door. I pulled the bell out hard and heard it jangle through the house.

Those few moments I stood waiting outside in the cold darkness were, I now realise, the last truly calm and untroubled ones I was ever to spend. Never again did I feel so steady and equable, never again did I anticipate nothing ahead of me of a frightening, unnerving and inexplicable kind. After this, I would be anxious and apprehensive no matter where I was or what I did. That something terrible, though I never knew what, was about to happen, in the next few moments, or hours, or days, I was always certain. I did not sleep well again, and if I feared for my own health and sanity, how much more did I fear for those of my family.

The front door opened. Leonora was standing there and in the poor light of the hall she looked far older, less smart, less assured, than she had ever been. When she held the door open for me in silence, and I stepped inside, I could see her better and my first impression was strengthened. The old Leonora had been well-dressed and groomed, elegant, sophisticated, hard, someone whose expression veered between fury and defiance, with an occasional prolonged sulkiness.

Tonight, she looked ten years older, was without make-up and her hair rolled into a loose bun at the back of her neck was thickly banded with grey. She seemed exhausted, her eyes oddly without expression, and her dress was plain, black, unbecoming.

'I hope I haven't startled you. I don't imagine you get many night callers. I did try to call you.'

'The phone is out of service. You'd better come into the kitchen. I can make tea. Or there might be a drink in the house somewhere.'

I followed her across the hall. Nothing seemed to have changed. The old furniture, pictures, curtains, carpet were still in place, as if they were everlasting and could never be worn out.

'Frederica is in here. It's the warmest room. I can't afford to heat the whole house.'

We went down the short passageway to the kitchen. It was dimly lit. Electricity was expensive.

'Frederica, stand up please. Here is a visitor.'

The child was seated at the kitchen table with her back to me. I saw that she looked tall for her age but extremely thin and that she had no hair and inevitably, the word 'cancer' came to me. She had had some terrible version of it and the treatment had made her bald and I felt sorry beyond expression, for her and for my cousin.

And then she got down from her chair, and turned to face me.

For a moment, I felt drained of all energy and consciousness, and almost reached out and grabbed the table to steady myself. But I knew that Leonora's eyes were on me, watching, watching, for just such a reaction, and so I managed to stay upright and clear-headed.

Frederica was about three years old but the face she presented to me now was the face of a wizened old woman. She had a long neck, and her mouth was misshapen, sucked inwards like that of an old person without teeth. Her eyes protruded slightly, and she had almost no lashes. Her hands were wrinkled and gnarled at the joints, as if she were ninety years old.

'There is no treatment and no cure.'

Leonora's voice was as matter-of-fact as if she had been giving me the name of a plant.

I did not want to stare at the child, but I shuddered to look at her. There was something alien about her. I have never had any reaction to a human being with a disfigurement or disease other than extreme sympathy and it has always seemed best to try to ignore the outward signs as quickly as possible and address the human being within. But this was so very different. I felt the usual recoil, shock, pity but far, far more strongly, I felt fear, fear and horror. Because this small child had aged in the way the china doll had aged. And insane and irrational as it seemed, I had no doubt she had aged because of it. The consequences of Leonora's violent temper and cruel, spiteful, destructive action all those years ago had come home to her now.

\* \* \*

I did not want to stay at Iyot House. I had a drink and read a picture book to the little girl, saddened when Leonora told me in bitterness that she would not live beyond the age of ten or so. She was a happy, friendly child with the happy chatter of a three year old coming so oddly out of that wizened little body.

As I was leaving, Leonora asked me to wait in the porch. The child had been left playing with a jigsaw in the kitchen, where I gathered they spent much of their time, because the rest of the house was so cold and unwelcoming, though I thought that she might have made it more cheerful if she had tried.

She came downstairs and handed me the cardboard box which I had left.

'Take it,' she said, 'hideous thing. What possessed you to leave such a thing here?'

'I – It seemed the right place for it, now there is a child here. Could Frederica not play with it?'

Leonora's face was pinched with a mixture of anger and scorn.

'Get rid of it, for God's sake. Haven't you done enough harm?'

'I? What harm have I done? You were the one who hurled the doll against the fireplace and smashed its head open, you were the one who caused . . .'

I stopped. Whatever crazy imaginings I had ever had, I could not conceivably blame my cousin for bringing such a dreadful fate upon her own child. I had no idea how the face of the broken doll had apparently aged but it was inanimate. It could not extract revenge.

I took the box which Leonora was pushing at me, and went. The front door was slammed and bolted before I had reached the gate.

The inn at Cold Eeyle was as comfortable and snug as ever. I was given my old room, and after a stiff whisky, I dined and then slept well and left a happier man to drive back home the next morning.

# 20

How to tell the rest of my story? How to explain any of it? I prided myself on being a rational man, on having explained things clearly to myself and come to some understanding of the phenomenon of coincidence. I even studied it a little, via the books of those whose life's work it is, and discovered just how much that was once thought mystical, magical, mysterious, is perfectly easily explained by coincidence, whose arm stretches far further than most people would guess.

Is that how I explain away the hideous events of the next few years? Am I convinced by putting it all down to likely chance?

Of course I am not. Things had happened to me in the past which I had pushed out of mind, buried deep so that I did not need to remember them. I had known then that they were not easily explained away and that the emotions and fears, the forebodings and anxieties that overwhelmed me from time to time were fully justified. Strange and inexplicable things had happened, and hidden forces had shaped events for reasons I did not understand. I also remained certain that Leonora was the lightning conductor for all of them.

A little over a year after my last visit to Iyot House my wife Catherine gave birth to a daughter, whom we christened Viola Kestrel. When she was almost three my work took me to India, which I loved, but about which Catherine had mixed feelings. She found the heat and humidity intolerable and the extreme poverty distressed her. But she loved the inhabitants at once, and found much to do helping women and their children in a remote village, where there were no medical facilities and where clothes and people were washed in the great river that flowed through the area. Viola was adored by everyone, and was an easy, smiling child, content to be petted and fussed by a dozen people in succession.

And then she was struck down within a few hours by one of the terrible diseases that ravage this beautiful country. Poor sanitation, contaminated water, easy spread of infection, any or all of them were to blame and in spite of Catherine's care and strict precautions it was perhaps a miracle that the child had not suffered from anything serious earlier.

Viola was very ill indeed, with a high fever, pains in her limbs and an intolerance of light. She was delirious and in great distress and we were in an agony of fear that we would lose her. On the fourth day, she woke with a rash of pox-like spots, raised, and red, all over her face and body. The spots were inflamed and became infected and scabbed, so that her fresh skin and beautiful features were hidden. After a week, handfuls of her beautiful corn-coloured hair began to fall out and did not regrow. She was a distressing sight and I think I was the one who felt the loss of her beauty the most. Catherine was absorbed in trying to nurse her, help her struggle through the fevers and relieve her symptoms, and so far as she was concerned that Viola should live, no matter what her eventual condition, was all she asked.

She did live. Slowly the fevers subsided and then ceased, her pain and discomfort eased, and she lay, limp and exhausted but out of danger, on a bed as cool as could be made for her, in a darkened corner. Her rash was less red and raised, but the hideous spots crusted and when they fell off left ugly pockmarks which were deep and unlikely ever to disappear. Her beautiful eyes were dimmed and lost their wonderful colour and translucence and seemed to have receded deep into their sockets.

Weeks and then three months went by before she

began to regain energy and a little weight, to laugh sometimes and clap her hands when the Indian women who had agonised over her clapped theirs.

We returned home exhausted and chastened, wondering what the future held for our once-perfect daughter, still perfect to us, still overwhelmingly loved, but nevertheless, sadly disfigured. In London we consulted a specialist in tropical diseases, who in turn passed us to a dermatologist, and thence to a plastic surgeon. None of them held out any hope that Viola's scars would ever fade very much. It might be possible for her to have a skin graft when she was older but success was by no means certain and there were risks.

Weeks went by while all this was attended to and we settled back with some difficulty into our old life in England.

It was then that I started to search for some particular files and in hunting, found both these and a white cardboard box. At first I did not recognise it and assumed it belonged to Catherine. I set it down on my work table, beside some drawings, but then forgot it until the following day, when I walked into my office early in the morning and as I saw it, remembered immediately where it had come from and what it held.

I saw Leonora again, in the semi-darkness outside Iyot House, thrusting the box into my hands and telling me, almost screaming at me to take it away. Well, my Viola might enjoy the Indian Princess doll, would recognise it as one of her friends and playmates from the country she still remembered vividly. I untied the loosely knotted string and lifted the lid. The rustle of the tissue paper brought goose flesh up on the back of my neck. It was not a sound I would ever again find pleasant and I pushed it aside quickly, not even liking the feel of it against my fingers.

The Indian Princess doll lay as I remembered her in the bottom of the coffin-like cardboard box. Her elaborate, richly embroidered and bejewelled clothes, her rings, earrings, bracelets and bangles and beads, her satin and lace and gold and silver braid and trim, were all as I had remembered them. There were just two things that were so very different.

Her thick long black hair had come away here and there, leaving ugly bald patches, and the fallen hair was lying in tufts at the bottom of the box.

And her face and hands, which were all that showed of her skin, were covered in deep and hideous pock-marks and scars. She was no longer a beauty, she was no longer about to be a bride, she was a pariah, a sufferer from a disfiguring disease which would mark her for life, someone from whom everyone turned away, their eyes downcast.